HERGÉ

THE ADVENTURES OF TINTIN

EXPLORERS ON THE MOON

LITTLE, BROWN AND COMPANY

BOSTON/NEW YORK/TORONTO/LONDON

Translated by Leslie Lonsdale-Cooper
and Michael Turner

The TINTIN books are published in the following languages :

Afrikaans :		HUMAN & ROUSSEAU, Cape Town.
Arabic :		DAR AL-MAAREF, Cairo.
Basque :		MENSAJERO, Bilbao.
Brazilian :		DISTRIBUIDORA RECORD, Rio de Janeiro.
Breton :		CASTERMAN, Paris.
Catalan :		JUVENTUD, Barcelona.
Chinese :		EPOCH, Taipei.
Danish :		CARLSEN IF, Copenhagen.
Dutch :		CASTERMAN, Dronten.
English :	U.K. :	METHUEN CHILDREN'S BOOKS, London.
	Australia :	REED PUBLISHING AUSTRALIA, Melbourne.
	Canada :	REED PUBLISHING CANADA, Toronto.
	New Zealand :	REED PUBLISHING NEW ZEALAND, Auckland.
	Republic of South Africa :	STRUIK BOOK DISTRIBUTORS, Johannesburg.
	Singapore :	REED PUBLISHING ASIA, Singapore.
	Spain :	EDICIONES DEL PRADO, Madrid.
	Portugal :	EDICIONES DEL PRADO, Madrid.
	U.S.A.	LITTLE BROWN, Boston.
Esperanto :		CASTERMAN, Paris.
Finnish :		OTAVA, Helsinki.
French :		CASTERMAN, Paris-Tournai.
	Spain :	EDICIONES DEL PRADO, Madrid.
	Portugal :	EDICIONES DEL PRADO, Madrid.
Galician :		JUVENTUD, Barcelona.
German :		CARLSEN, Reinbek-Hamburg.
Greek :		ANGLO-HELLENIC, Athens.
Icelandic :		FJÖLVI, Reykjavik.
Indonesian :		INDIRA, Jakarta.
Iranian :		MODERN PRINTING HOUSE, Teheran.
Italian :		GANDUS, Genoa.
Japanese :		FUKUINKAN SHOTEN, Tokyo.
Korean :		UNIVERSAL PUBLICATIONS, Seoul.
Malay :		SHARIKAT UNITED, Pulau Pinang.
Norwegian :		SEMIC, Oslo.
Picard :		CASTERMAN, Paris.
Portuguese :		CENTRO DO LIVRO BRASILEIRO, Lisboa.
Provençal :		CASTERMAN, Paris.
Spanish :		JUVENTUD, Barcelona.
	Argentina :	JUVENTUD ARGENTINA, Buenos Aires.
	Mexico :	MARIN, Mexico.
	Peru :	DISTR. DE LIBROS DEL PACIFICO, Lima.
Serbo-Croatian :		DECJE NOVINE, Gornji Milanovac.
Swedish :		CARLSEN IF, Stockholm.
Welsh :		GWASG Y DREF WEN, Cardiff.

Artwork © 1954 by Casterman, Paris and Tournai
Library of Congress Catalogue Card Number Afo 17608
© renewed 1982 by Casterman
Library of Congress Catalogue Card Number R 122385
Translation Text © 1959 by Methuen & Co., Ltd., London
American Edition © 1976 by Little, Brown and Company (Inc.), Boston

Library of Congress catalog card no. 76-13297

20 19

Published pursuant to agreement with Casterman, Paris
Not for sale in the British Commonwealth

Printed in Belgium by Casterman Printers s.a., Tournai

EXPLORERS ON THE MOON

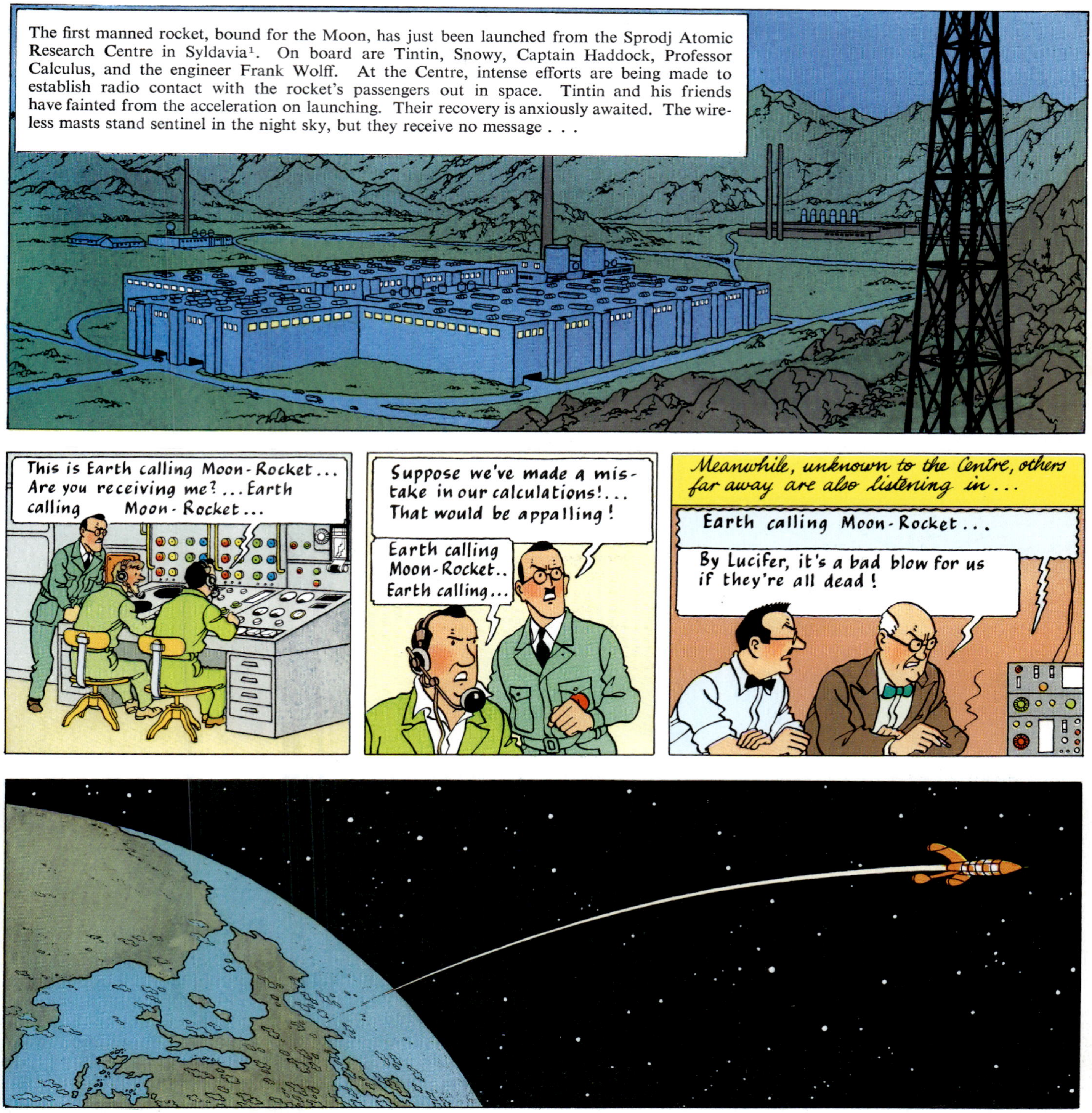
The first manned rocket, bound for the Moon, has just been launched from the Sprodj Atomic Research Centre in Syldavia[1]. On board are Tintin, Snowy, Captain Haddock, Professor Calculus, and the engineer Frank Wolff. At the Centre, intense efforts are being made to establish radio contact with the rocket's passengers out in space. Tintin and his friends have fainted from the acceleration on launching. Their recovery is anxiously awaited. The wireless masts stand sentinel in the night sky, but they receive no message . . .
This is Earth calling Moon-Rocket ... Are you receiving me? ... Earth calling Moon-Rocket ...
Suppose we've made a mistake in our calculations!... That would be appalling!
Earth calling Moon-Rocket.. Earth calling...
Meanwhile, unknown to the Centre, others far away are also listening in ...
Earth calling Moon-Rocket ...
By Lucifer, it's a bad blow for us if they're all dead!

[1] See Destination Moon

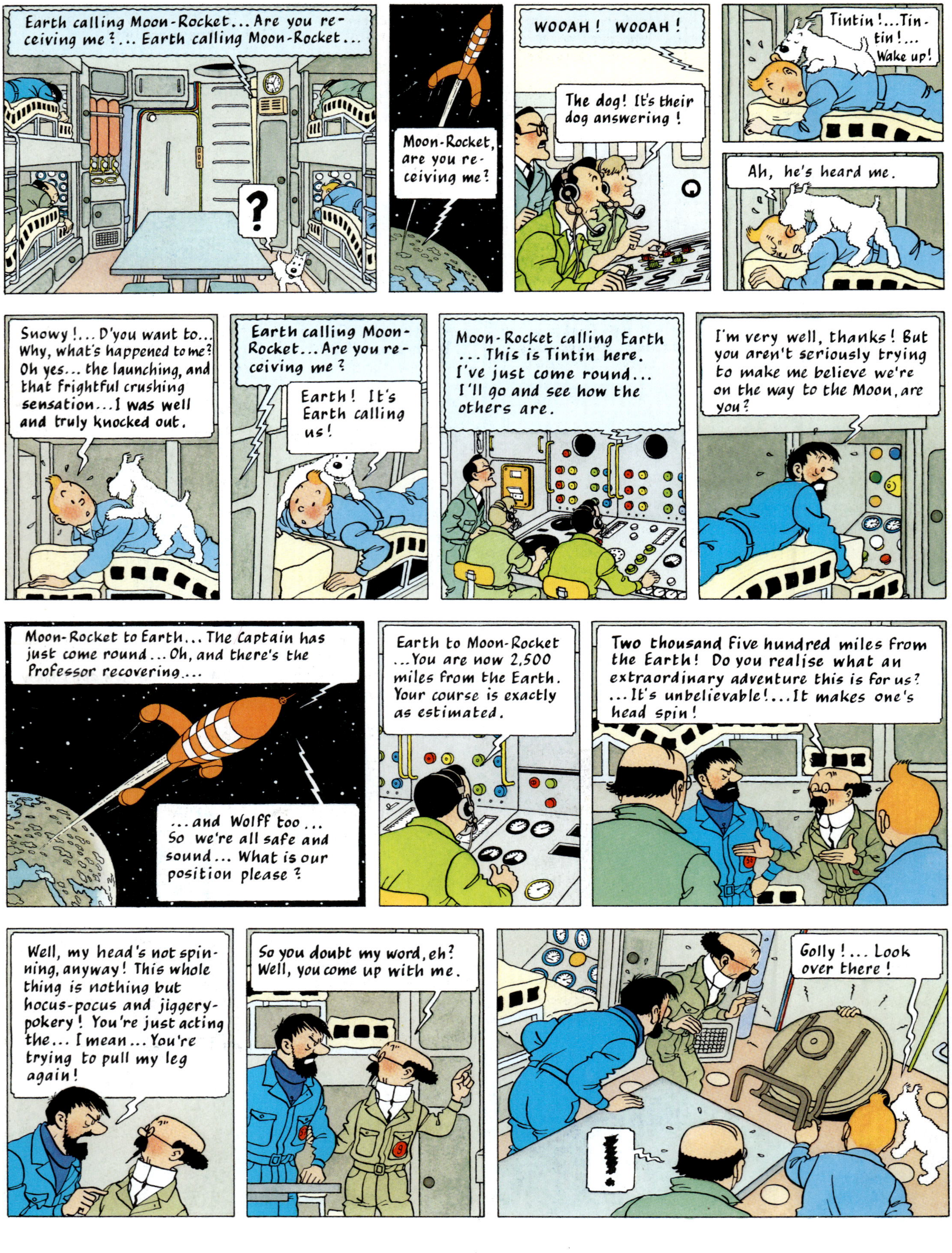

Earth calling Moon-Rocket... Are you receiving me?... Earth calling Moon-Rocket...
?
Moon-Rocket, are you receiving me?
WOOAH! WOOAH!
The dog! It's their dog answering!
Tintin!... Tintin!... Wake up!
Ah, he's heard me.
Snowy!... D'you want to... Why, what's happened to me? Oh yes... the launching, and that frightful crushing sensation... I was well and truly knocked out.
Earth calling Moon-Rocket... Are you receiving me?
Earth! It's Earth calling us!
Moon-Rocket calling Earth... This is Tintin here. I've just come round... I'll go and see how the others are.
I'm very well, thanks! But you aren't seriously trying to make me believe we're on the way to the Moon, are you?
Moon-Rocket to Earth... The Captain has just come round... Oh, and there's the Professor recovering....
...and Wolff too... So we're all safe and sound... What is our position please?
Earth to Moon-Rocket ...You are now 2,500 miles from the Earth. Your course is exactly as estimated.
Two thousand five hundred miles from the Earth! Do you realise what an extraordinary adventure this is for us? ...It's unbelievable!... It makes one's head spin!
Well, my head's not spinning, anyway! This whole thing is nothing but hocus-pocus and jiggery-pokery! You're just acting the... I mean... You're trying to pull my leg again!
So you doubt my word, eh? Well, you come up with me.
Golly!... Look over there!
!

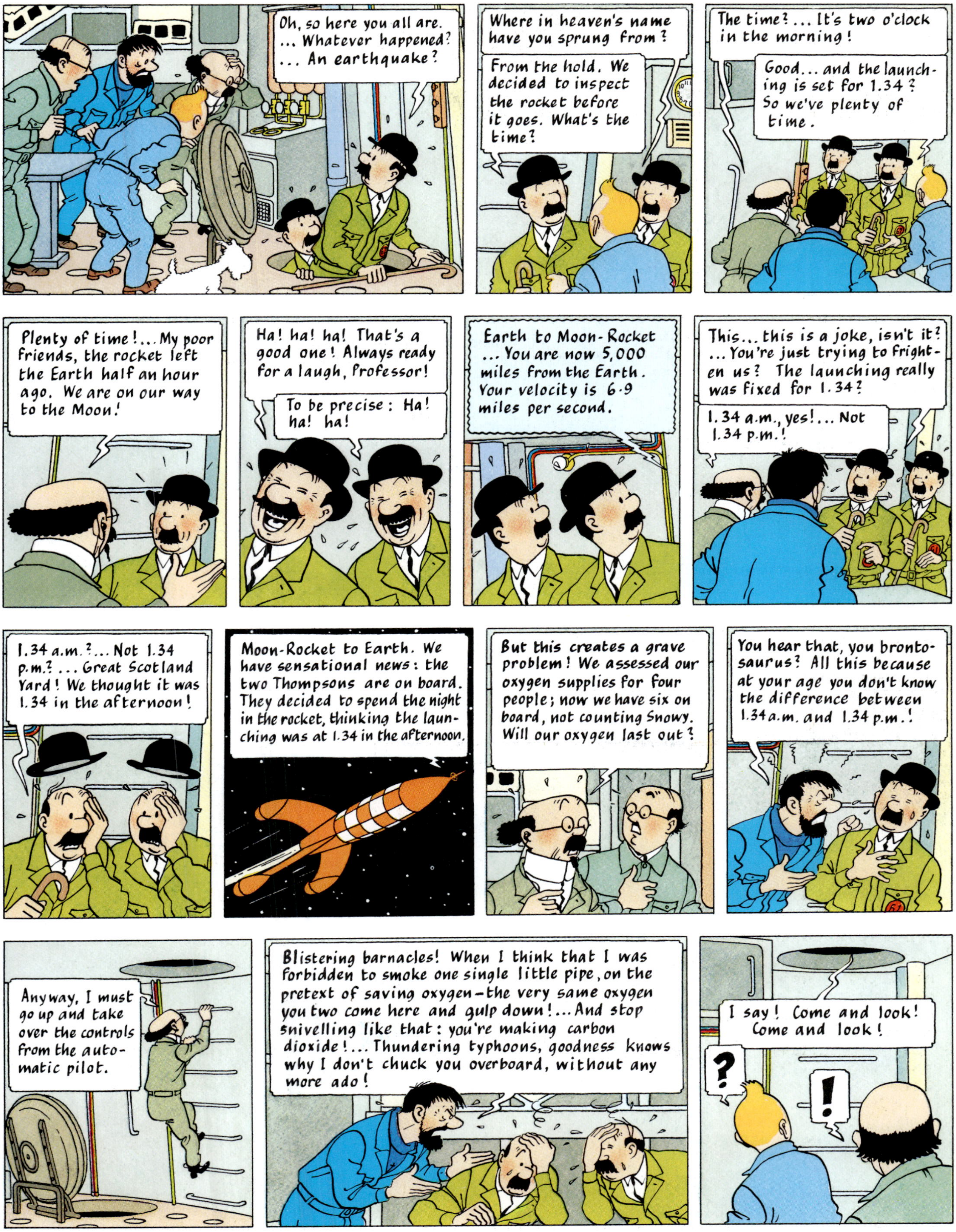
Oh, so here you all are. ... Whatever happened? ... An earthquake?
Where in heaven's name have you sprung from?
From the hold. We decided to inspect the rocket before it goes. What's the time?
The time? ... It's two o'clock in the morning!
Good... and the launching is set for 1.34? So we've plenty of time.
Plenty of time!... My poor friends, the rocket left the Earth half an hour ago. We are on our way to the Moon!
Ha! ha! ha! That's a good one! Always ready for a laugh, Professor!
To be precise: Ha! ha! ha!
Earth to Moon-Rocket ... You are now 5,000 miles from the Earth. Your velocity is 6·9 miles per second.
This... this is a joke, isn't it? ... You're just trying to frighten us? The launching really was fixed for 1.34?
1.34 a.m., yes!... Not 1.34 p.m.!
1.34 a.m.?... Not 1.34 p.m.? ... Great Scotland Yard! We thought it was 1.34 in the afternoon!
Moon-Rocket to Earth. We have sensational news: the two Thompsons are on board. They decided to spend the night in the rocket, thinking the launching was at 1.34 in the afternoon.
But this creates a grave problem! We assessed our oxygen supplies for four people; now we have six on board, not counting Snowy. Will our oxygen last out?
You hear that, you brontosaurus? All this because at your age you don't know the difference between 1.34 a.m. and 1.34 p.m.!
Anyway, I must go up and take over the controls from the automatic pilot.
Blistering barnacles! When I think that I was forbidden to smoke one single little pipe, on the pretext of saving oxygen—the very same oxygen you two come here and gulp down!... And stop snivelling like that: you're making carbon dioxide!... Thundering typhoons, goodness knows why I don't chuck you overboard, without any more ado!
I say! Come and look! Come and look!
?
!

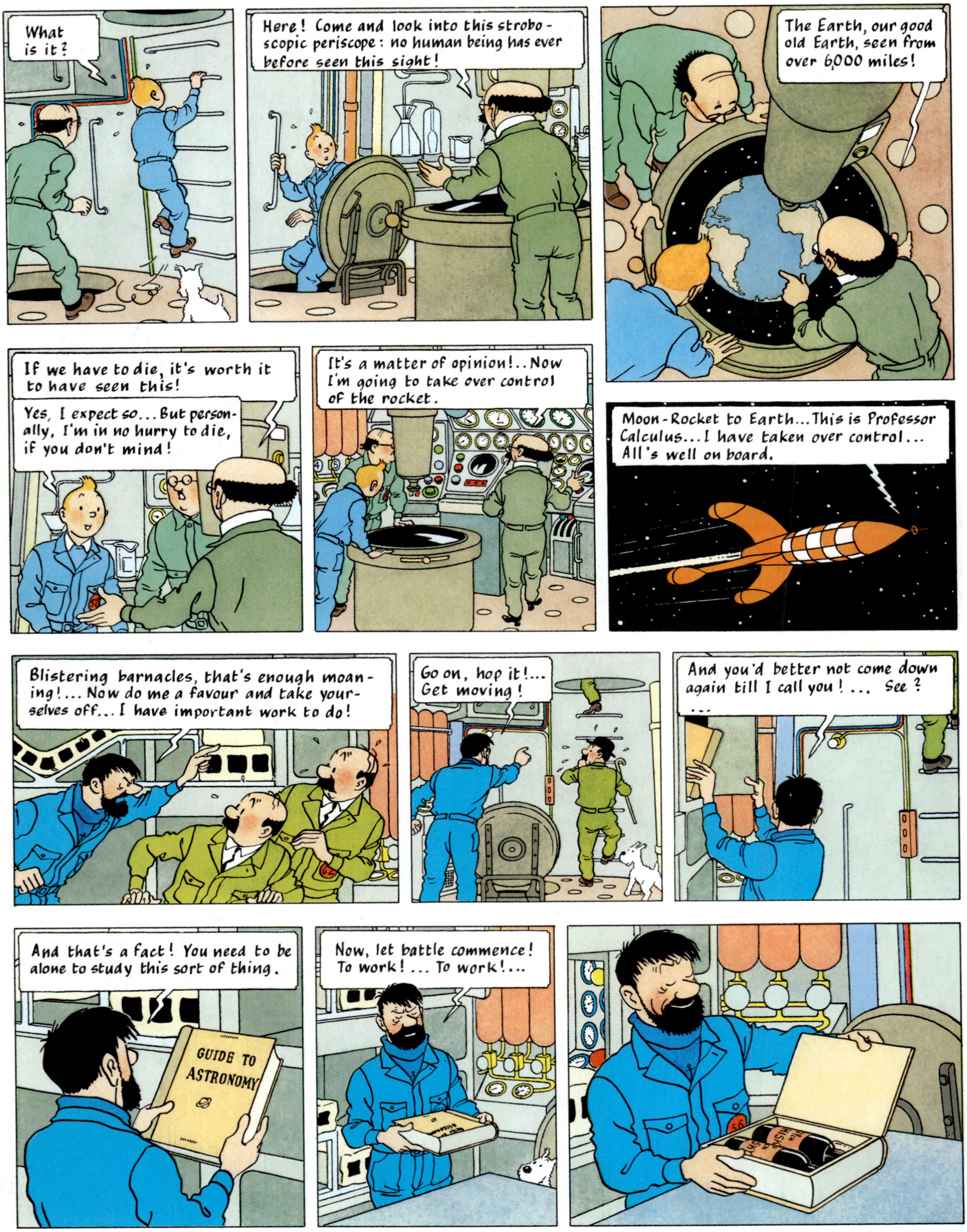
What is it?
Here! Come and look into this stroboscopic periscope: no human being has ever before seen this sight!
The Earth, our good old Earth, seen from over 6,000 miles!
If we have to die, it's worth it to have seen this!
Yes, I expect so... But personally, I'm in no hurry to die, if you don't mind!
It's a matter of opinion!.. Now I'm going to take over control of the rocket.
Moon-Rocket to Earth... This is Professor Calculus... I have taken over control... All's well on board.
Blistering barnacles, that's enough moaning!... Now do me a favour and take yourselves off... I have important work to do!
Go on, hop it!... Get moving!
And you'd better not come down again till I call you!... See?...
And that's a fact! You need to be alone to study this sort of thing.
GUIDE TO ASTRONOMY
Now, let battle commence! To work!... To work!...

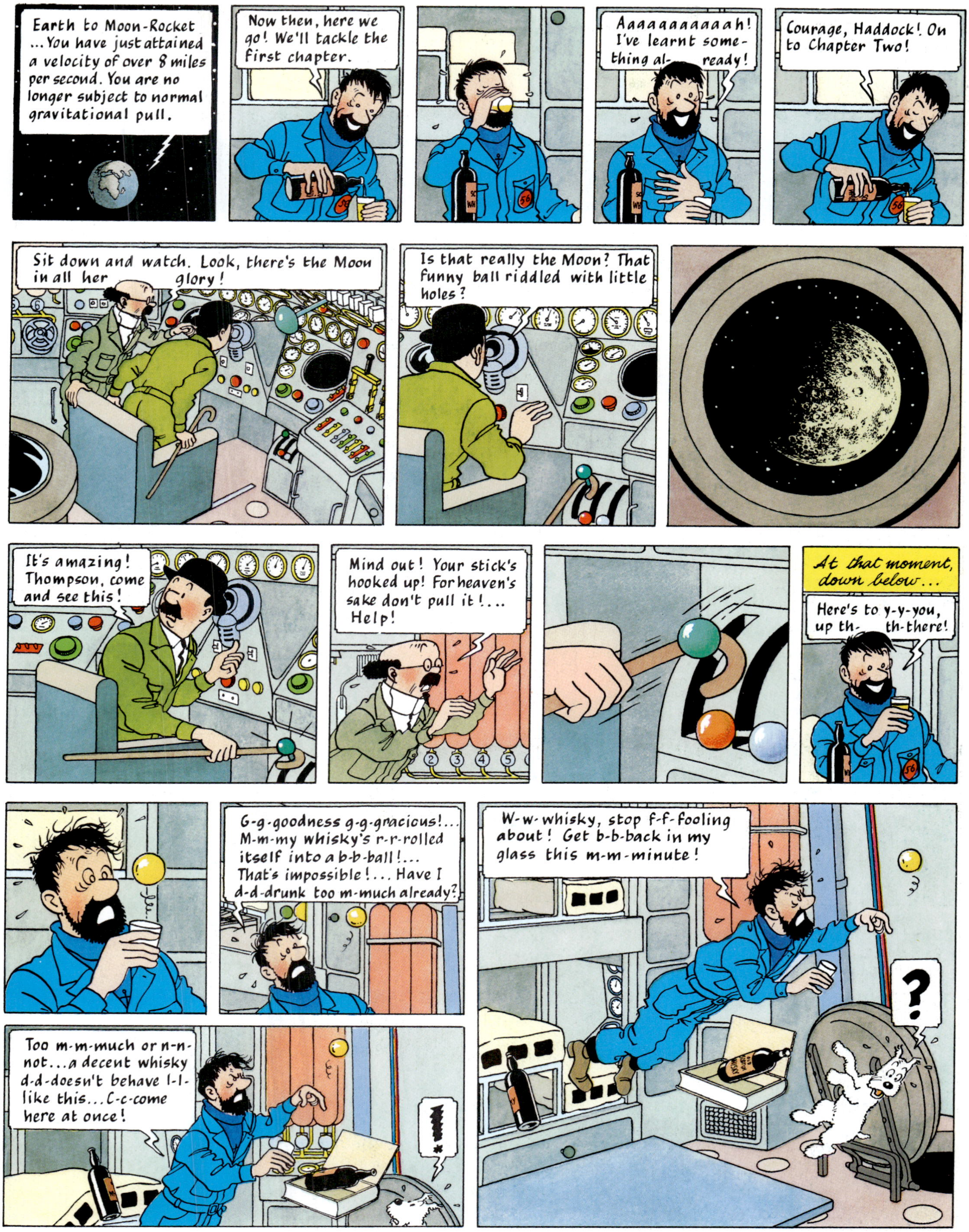
Earth to Moon-Rocket ...You have just attained a velocity of over 8 miles per second. You are no longer subject to normal gravitational pull.
Now then, here we go! We'll tackle the first chapter.
Aaaaaaaaaaah! I've learnt something al- ready!
Courage, Haddock! On to Chapter Two!
Sit down and watch. Look, there's the Moon in all her glory!
Is that really the Moon? That funny ball riddled with little holes?
It's amazing! Thompson, come and see this!
Mind out! Your stick's hooked up! For heaven's sake don't pull it!... Help!
At that moment, down below...
Here's to y-y-you, up th- th-there!
G-g-goodness g-g-gracious!... M-m-my whisky's r-r-rolled itself into a b-b-ball!... That's impossible!... Have I d-d-drunk too m-much already?
W-w-whisky, stop f-f-fooling about! Get b-b-back in my glass this m-m-minute!
?
Too m-m-much or n-n-not...a decent whisky d-d-doesn't behave l-l-like this...C-c-come here at once!

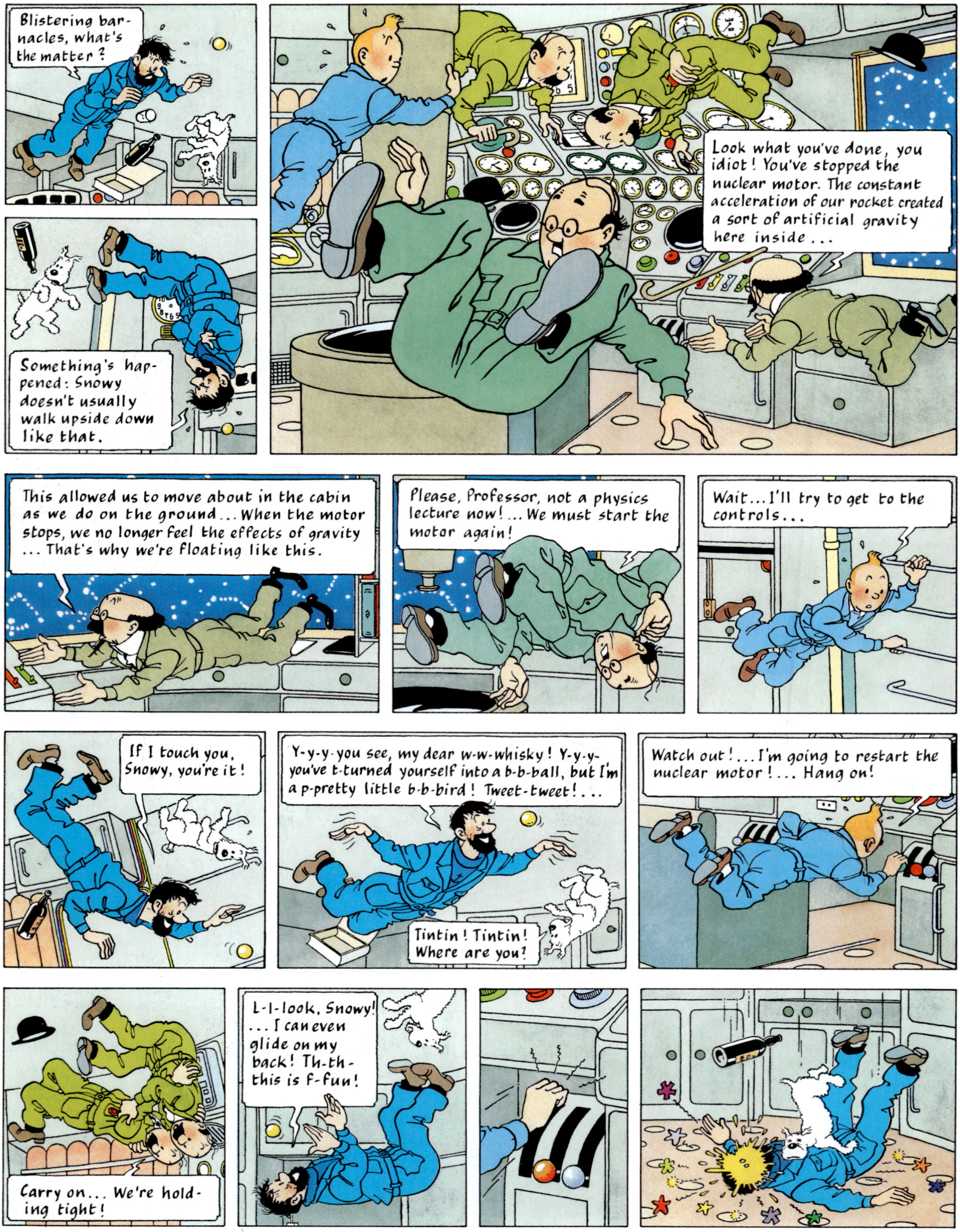
Blistering barnacles, what's the matter?
Look what you've done, you idiot! You've stopped the nuclear motor. The constant acceleration of our rocket created a sort of artificial gravity here inside...
Something's happened: Snowy doesn't usually walk upside down like that.
This allowed us to move about in the cabin as we do on the ground... When the motor stops, we no longer feel the effects of gravity... That's why we're floating like this.
Please, Professor, not a physics lecture now!... We must start the motor again!
Wait... I'll try to get to the controls...
If I touch you, Snowy, you're it!
Y-y-y-you see, my dear w-w-whisky! Y-y-y-you've t-turned yourself into a b-b-ball, but I'm a p-pretty little b-b-bird! Tweet-tweet!...
Tintin! Tintin! Where are you?
Watch out!... I'm going to restart the nuclear motor!... Hang on!
Carry on... We're holding tight!
L-l-look, Snowy!... I can even glide on my back! Th-th-this is f-fun!

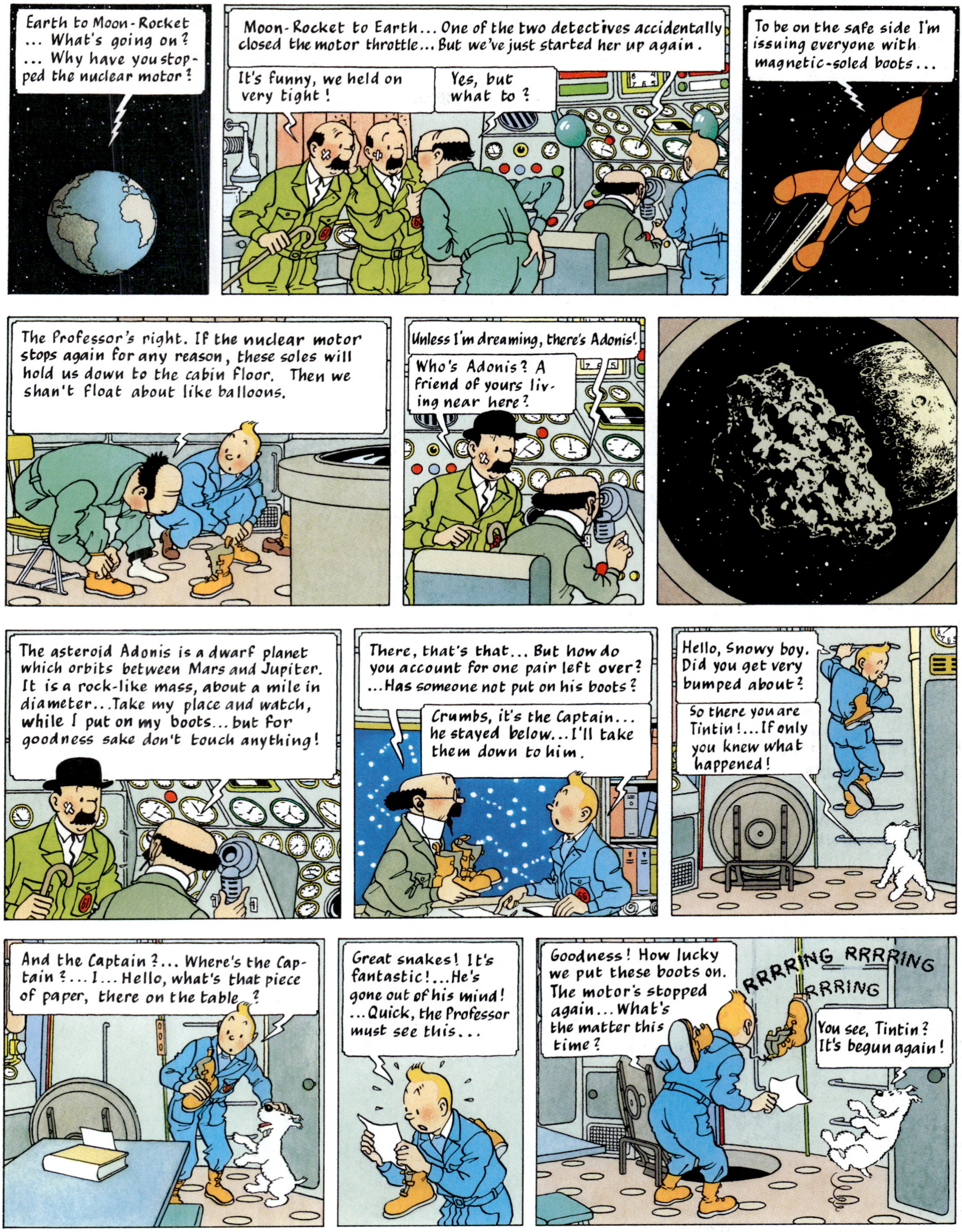
Earth to Moon-Rocket ... What's going on? ... Why have you stopped the nuclear motor?
Moon-Rocket to Earth... One of the two detectives accidentally closed the motor throttle... But we've just started her up again.
It's funny, we held on very tight!
Yes, but what to?
To be on the safe side I'm issuing everyone with magnetic-soled boots...
The Professor's right. If the nuclear motor stops again for any reason, these soles will hold us down to the cabin floor. Then we shan't float about like balloons.
Unless I'm dreaming, there's Adonis!
Who's Adonis? A friend of yours living near here?
The asteroid Adonis is a dwarf planet which orbits between Mars and Jupiter. It is a rock-like mass, about a mile in diameter... Take my place and watch, while I put on my boots... but for goodness sake don't touch anything!
There, that's that... But how do you account for one pair left over? ...Has someone not put on his boots?
Crumbs, it's the Captain... he stayed below... I'll take them down to him.
Hello, Snowy boy. Did you get very bumped about?
So there you are Tintin!... If only you knew what happened!
And the Captain?... Where's the Captain?... I... Hello, what's that piece of paper, there on the table...?
Great snakes! It's fantastic!... He's gone out of his mind! ...Quick, the Professor must see this...
Goodness! How lucky we put these boots on. The motor's stopped again... What's the matter this time?
RRRRING RRRRING
RRRING
You see, Tintin? It's begun again!

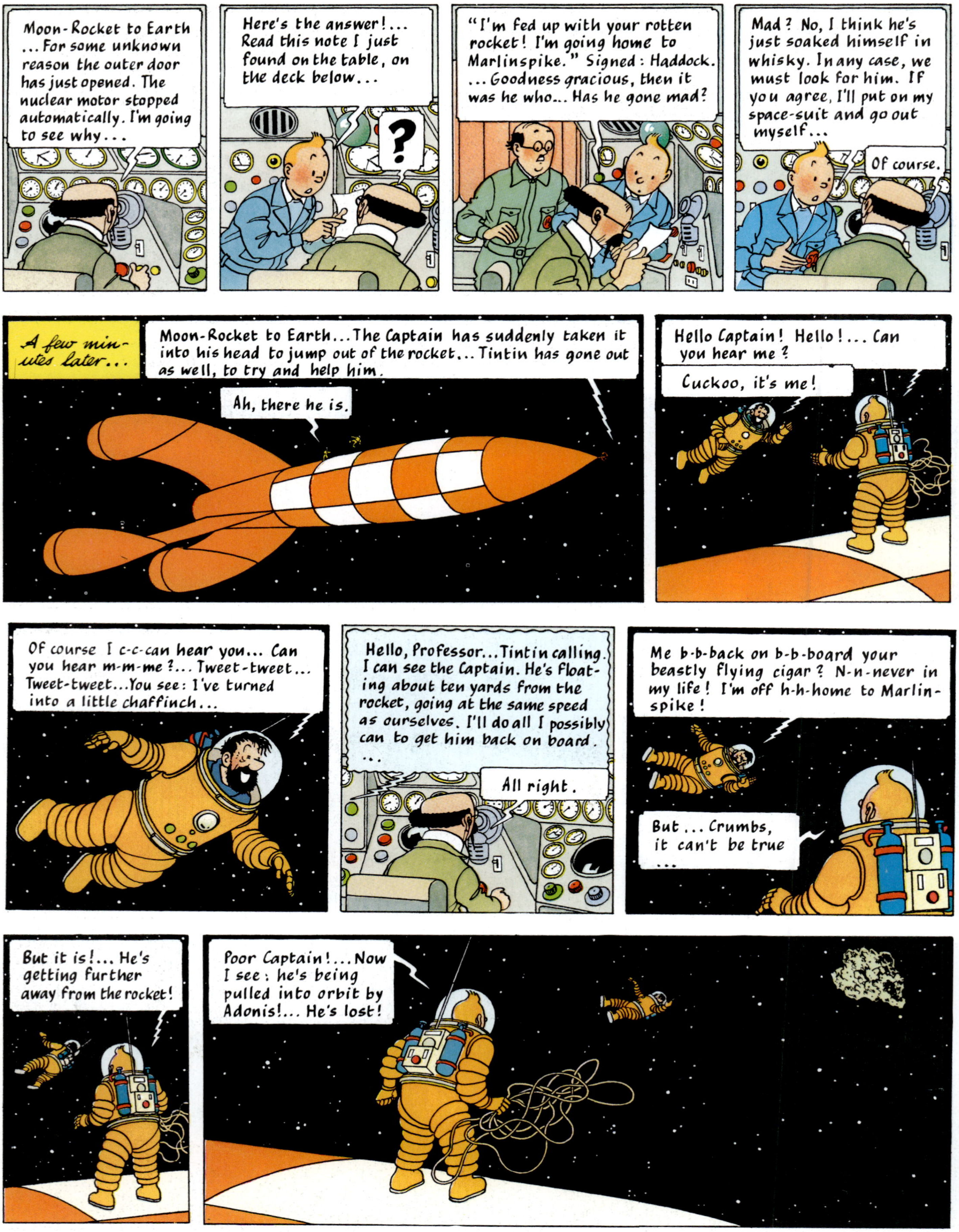

Moon-Rocket to Earth ... For some unknown reason the outer door has just opened. The nuclear motor stopped automatically. I'm going to see why...
Here's the answer!... Read this note I just found on the table, on the deck below...
?
"I'm fed up with your rotten rocket! I'm going home to Marlinspike." Signed: Haddock. ... Goodness gracious, then it was he who... Has he gone mad?
Mad? No, I think he's just soaked himself in whisky. In any case, we must look for him. If you agree, I'll put on my space-suit and go out myself...
Of course.
A few minutes later...
Moon-Rocket to Earth... The Captain has suddenly taken it into his head to jump out of the rocket... Tintin has gone out as well, to try and help him.
Ah, there he is.
Hello Captain! Hello!... Can you hear me?
Cuckoo, it's me!
Of course I c-c-can hear you... Can you hear m-m-me?... Tweet-tweet... Tweet-tweet... You see: I've turned into a little chaffinch...
Hello, Professor... Tintin calling. I can see the Captain. He's floating about ten yards from the rocket, going at the same speed as ourselves. I'll do all I possibly can to get him back on board. ...
All right.
Me b-b-back on b-b-board your beastly flying cigar? N-n-never in my life! I'm off h-h-home to Marlinspike!
But ... Crumbs, it can't be true ...
But it is!... He's getting further away from the rocket!
Poor Captain!... Now I see: he's being pulled into orbit by Adonis!... He's lost!

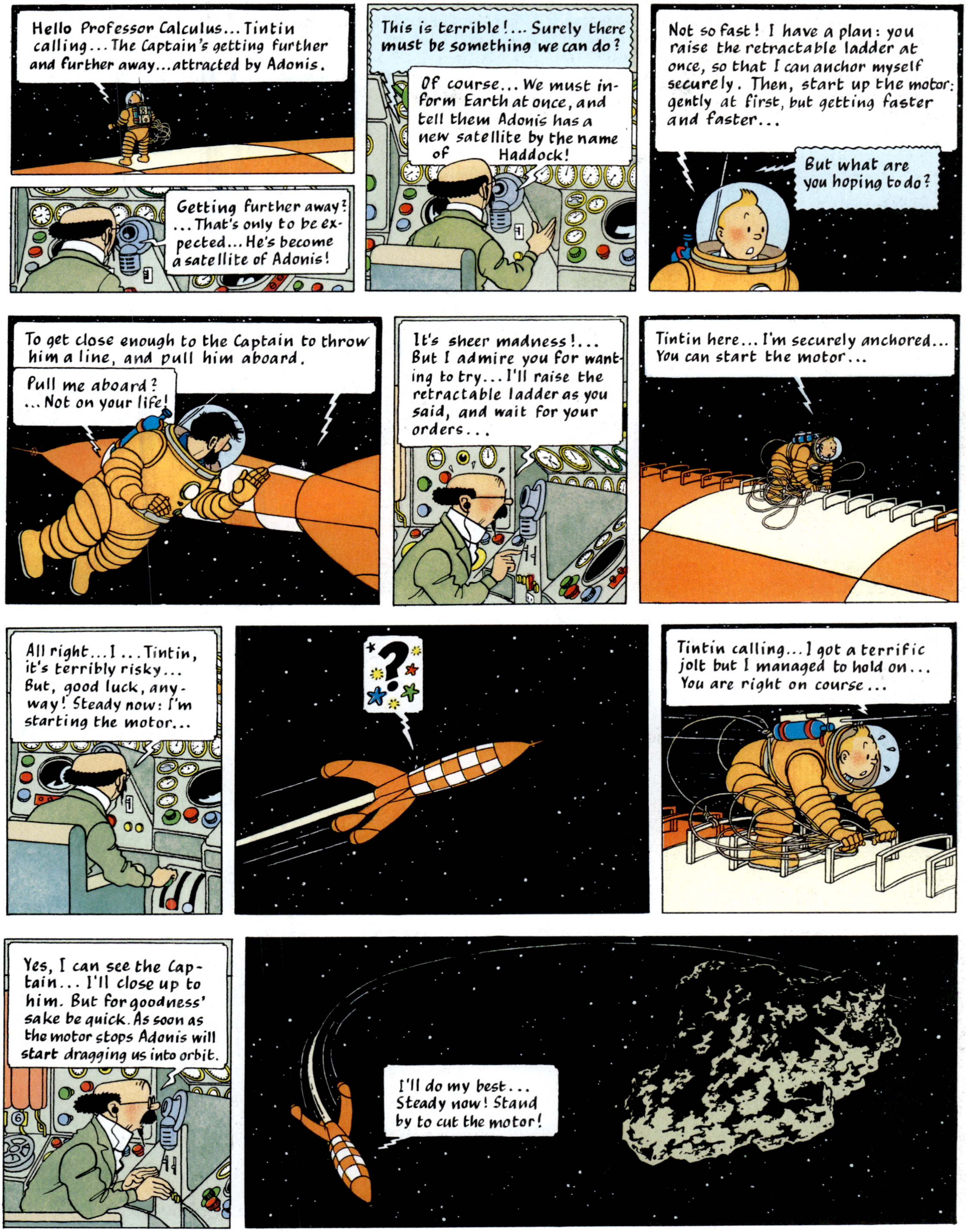
Hello Professor Calculus... Tintin calling... The Captain's getting further and further away... attracted by Adonis.
Getting further away? ...That's only to be expected... He's become a satellite of Adonis!
This is terrible!... Surely there must be something we can do?
Of course... We must inform Earth at once, and tell them Adonis has a new satellite by the name of Haddock!
Not so fast! I have a plan: you raise the retractable ladder at once, so that I can anchor myself securely. Then, start up the motor: gently at first, but getting faster and faster...
But what are you hoping to do?
To get close enough to the Captain to throw him a line, and pull him aboard.
Pull me aboard? ...Not on your life!
It's sheer madness!... But I admire you for wanting to try... I'll raise the retractable ladder as you said, and wait for your orders...
Tintin here... I'm securely anchored... You can start the motor...
All right... I... Tintin, it's terribly risky... But, good luck, anyway! Steady now: I'm starting the motor...
?
Tintin calling... I got a terrific jolt but I managed to hold on... You are right on course...
Yes, I can see the Captain... I'll close up to him. But for goodness' sake be quick. As soon as the motor stops Adonis will start dragging us into orbit.
I'll do my best... Steady now! Stand by to cut the motor!

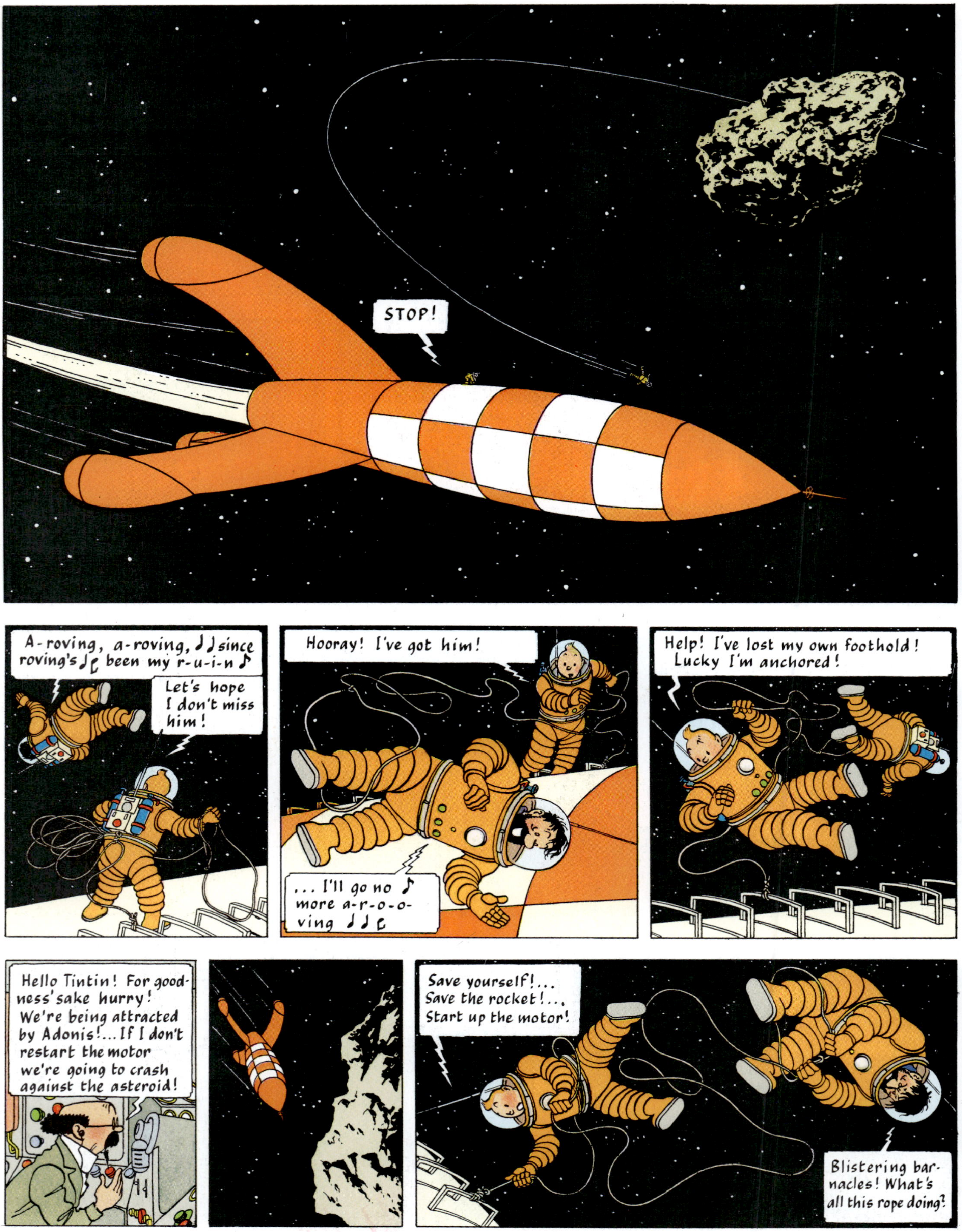
STOP!
A-roving, a-roving, ♪♪ since roving's ♪♪ been my r-u-i-n ♪
Let's hope I don't miss him!
Hooray! I've got him!
... I'll go no ♪ more a-r-o-o-ving ♪♪♪
Help! I've lost my own foothold! Lucky I'm anchored!
Hello Tintin! For goodness' sake hurry! We're being attracted by Adonis!... If I don't restart the motor we're going to crash against the asteroid!
Save yourself!... Save the rocket!... Start up the motor!
Blistering barnacles! What's all this rope doing?

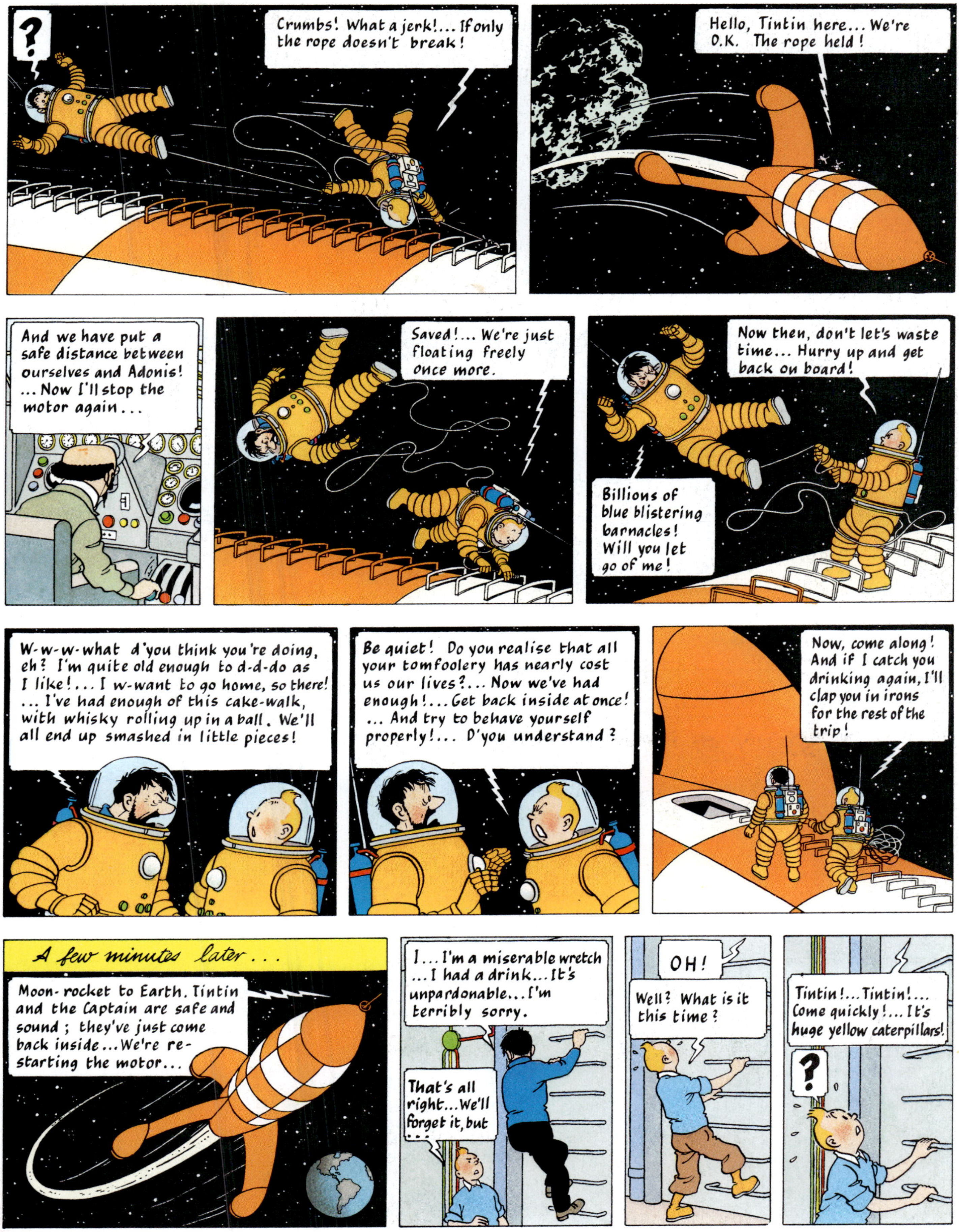
?
Crumbs! What a jerk!... If only the rope doesn't break!
Hello, Tintin here... We're O.K. The rope held!
And we have put a safe distance between ourselves and Adonis! ... Now I'll stop the motor again...
Saved!... We're just floating freely once more.
Now then, don't let's waste time... Hurry up and get back on board!
Billions of blue blistering barnacles! Will you let go of me!
W-w-w-what d'you think you're doing, eh? I'm quite old enough to d-d-do as I like!... I w-want to go home, so there! ... I've had enough of this cake-walk, with whisky rolling up in a ball. We'll all end up smashed in little pieces!
Be quiet! Do you realise that all your tomfoolery has nearly cost us our lives?... Now we've had enough!... Get back inside at once! ... And try to behave yourself properly!... D'you understand?
Now, come along! And if I catch you drinking again, I'll clap you in irons for the rest of the trip!
A few minutes later...
Moon-rocket to Earth. Tintin and the Captain are safe and sound; they've just come back inside... We're re-starting the motor...
I... I'm a miserable wretch ... I had a drink... It's unpardonable... I'm terribly sorry.
That's all right... We'll forget it, but ...
OH!
Well? What is it this time?
Tintin!... Tintin!... Come quickly!... It's huge yellow caterpillars!
?

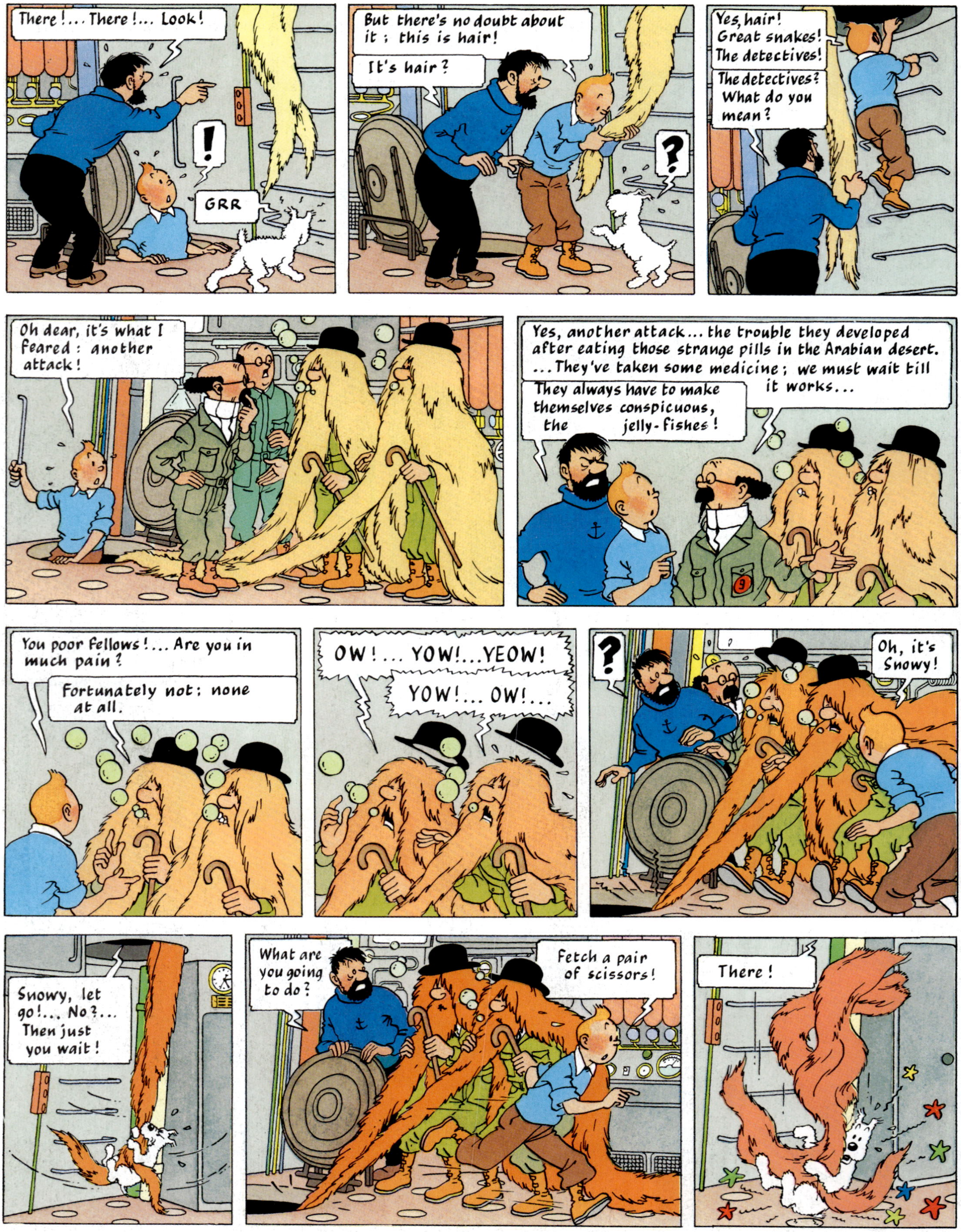

There!... There!... Look!
!
GRR
But there's no doubt about it: this is hair!
It's hair?
?
Yes, hair! Great snakes! The detectives!
The detectives? What do you mean?
Oh dear, it's what I feared: another attack!
Yes, another attack... the trouble they developed after eating those strange pills in the Arabian desert. ...They've taken some medicine; we must wait till it works...
They always have to make themselves conspicuous, the jelly-fishes!
You poor fellows!... Are you in much pain?
Fortunately not: none at all.
OW!... YOW!...YEOW!
YOW!... OW!...
?
Oh, it's Snowy!
Snowy, let go!... No?... Then just you wait!
What are you going to do?
Fetch a pair of scissors!
There!

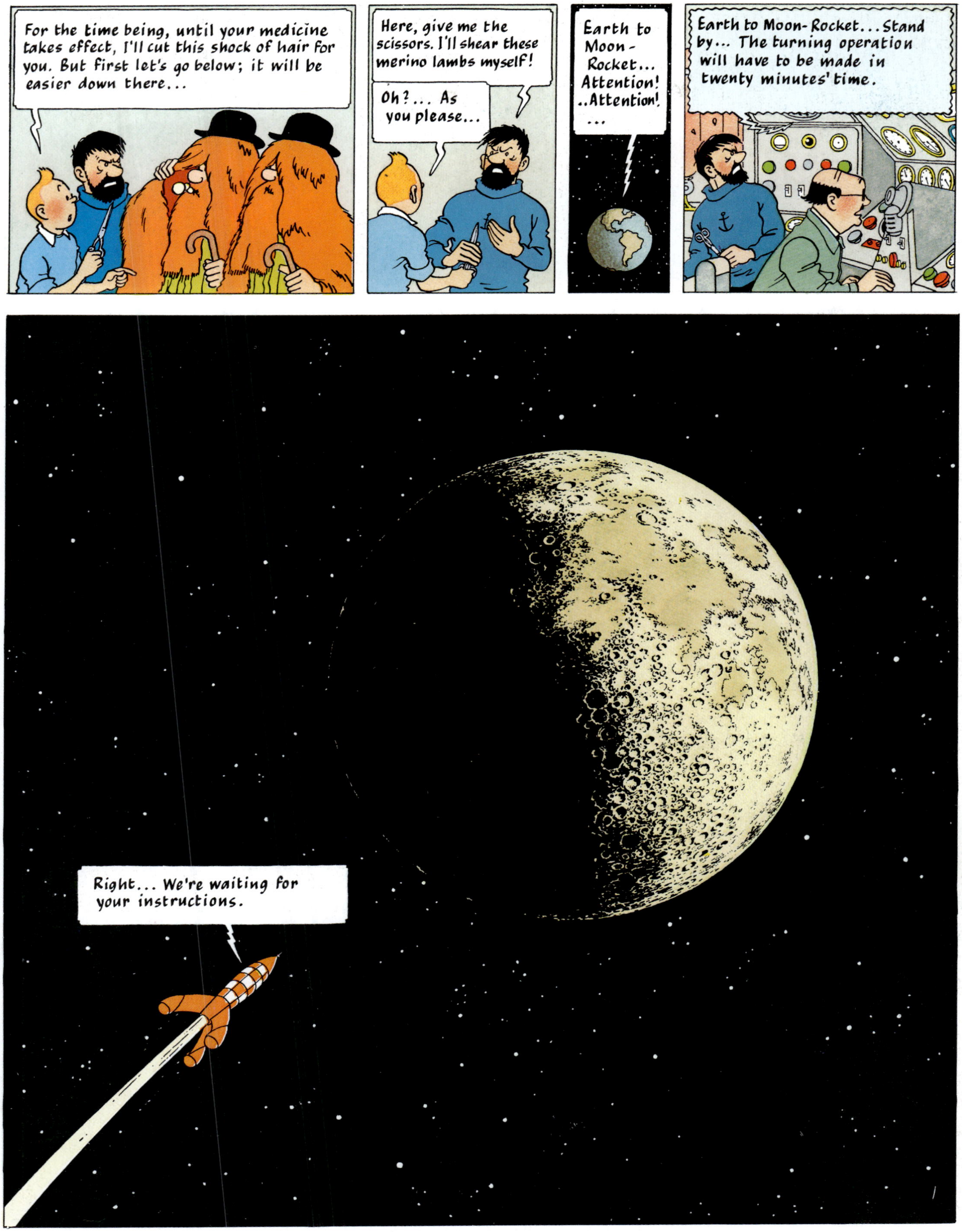
For the time being, until your medicine takes effect, I'll cut this shock of hair for you. But first let's go below; it will be easier down there...
Here, give me the scissors. I'll shear these merino lambs myself!
Oh?... As you please...
Earth to Moon-Rocket... Attention! ..Attention! ...
Earth to Moon-Rocket... Stand by... The turning operation will have to be made in twenty minutes' time.
Right... We're waiting for your instructions.

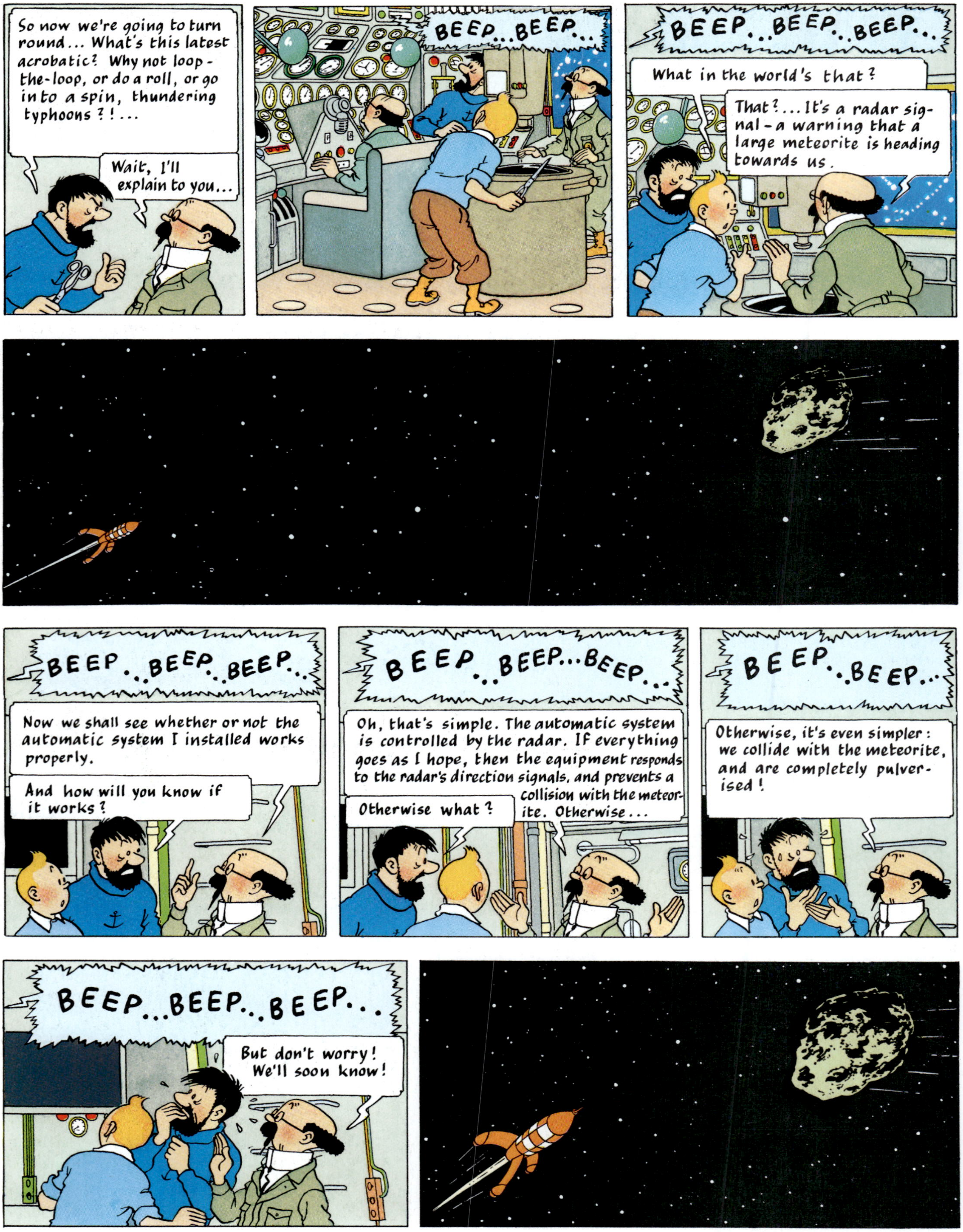
So now we're going to turn round... What's this latest acrobatic? Why not loop-the-loop, or do a roll, or go into a spin, thundering typhoons?!...
Wait, I'll explain to you...
BEEP...BEEP...
BEEP...BEEP...BEEP...
What in the world's that?
That?... It's a radar signal - a warning that a large meteorite is heading towards us.
BEEP...BEEP...BEEP...
Now we shall see whether or not the automatic system I installed works properly.
And how will you know if it works?
BEEP...BEEP...BEEP...
Oh, that's simple. The automatic system is controlled by the radar. If everything goes as I hope, then the equipment responds to the radar's direction signals, and prevents a collision with the meteorite. Otherwise...
Otherwise what?
BEEP...BEEP...
Otherwise, it's even simpler: we collide with the meteorite, and are completely pulverised!
BEEP...BEEP...BEEP...
But don't worry! We'll soon know!

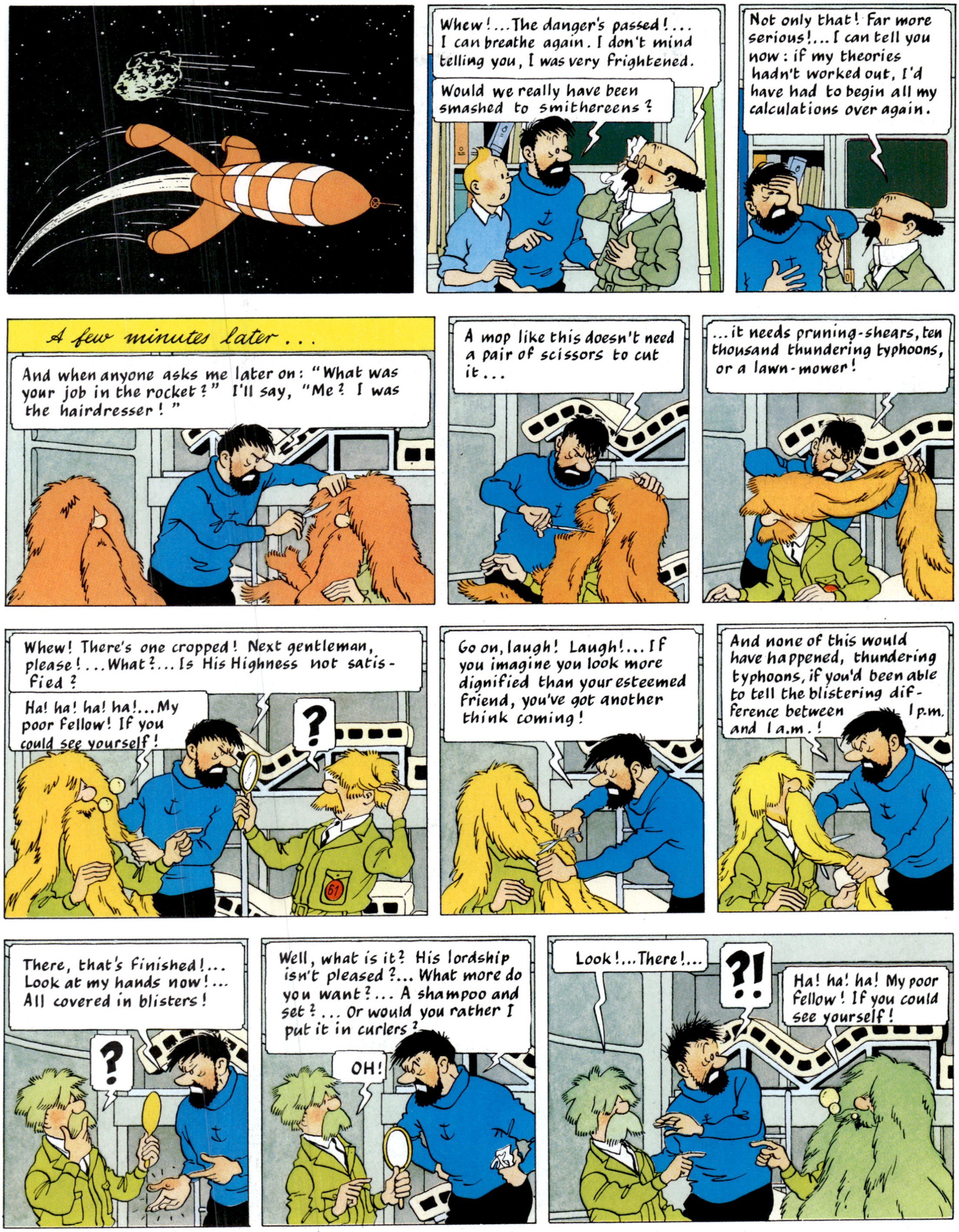

Whew!... The danger's passed!... I can breathe again. I don't mind telling you, I was very frightened.
Would we really have been smashed to smithereens?
Not only that! Far more serious!... I can tell you now: if my theories hadn't worked out, I'd have had to begin all my calculations over again.
A few minutes later...
And when anyone asks me later on: "What was your job in the rocket?" I'll say, "Me? I was the hairdresser!"
A mop like this doesn't need a pair of scissors to cut it...
...it needs pruning-shears, ten thousand thundering typhoons, or a lawn-mower!
Whew! There's one cropped! Next gentleman, please!... What?... Is His Highness not satisfied?
Ha! ha! ha! ha!... My poor fellow! If you could see yourself!
?
Go on, laugh! Laugh!... If you imagine you look more dignified than your esteemed friend, you've got another think coming!
And none of this would have happened, thundering typhoons, if you'd been able to tell the blistering difference between 1 p.m. and 1 a.m.!
There, that's finished!... Look at my hands now!... All covered in blisters!
?
Well, what is it? His lordship isn't pleased?... What more do you want?... A shampoo and set?... Or would you rather I put it in curlers?
OH!
Look!... There!...
?!
Ha! ha! ha! My poor fellow! If you could see yourself!

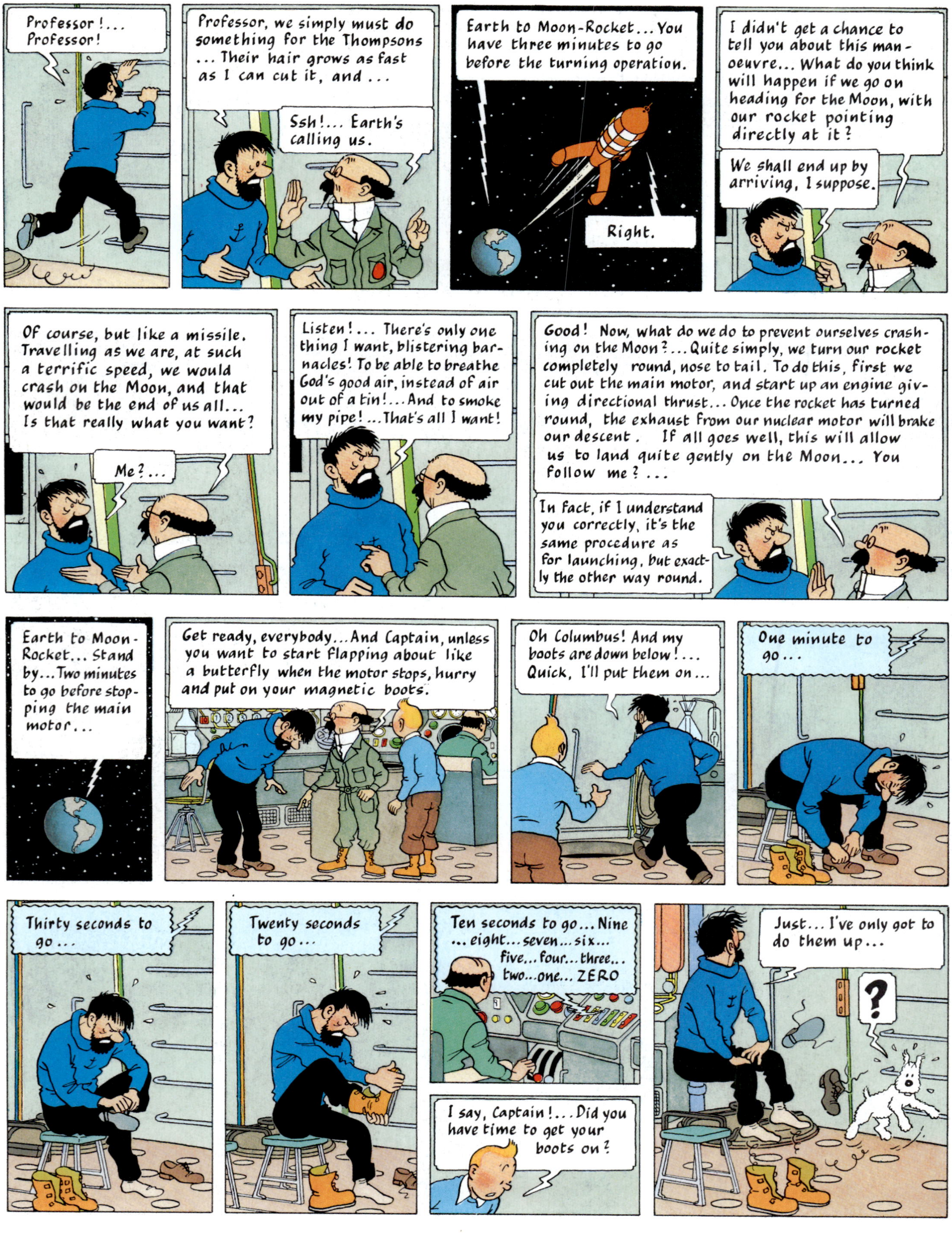
Professor!... Professor!
Professor, we simply must do something for the Thompsons ... Their hair grows as fast as I can cut it, and ...
Ssh!... Earth's calling us.
Earth to Moon-Rocket... You have three minutes to go before the turning operation.
Right.
I didn't get a chance to tell you about this manoeuvre... What do you think will happen if we go on heading for the Moon, with our rocket pointing directly at it?
We shall end up by arriving, I suppose.
Of course, but like a missile. Travelling as we are, at such a terrific speed, we would crash on the Moon, and that would be the end of us all... Is that really what you want?
Me?...
Listen!... There's only one thing I want, blistering barnacles! To be able to breathe God's good air, instead of air out of a tin!... And to smoke my pipe!... That's all I want!
Good! Now, what do we do to prevent ourselves crashing on the Moon?... Quite simply, we turn our rocket completely round, nose to tail. To do this, first we cut out the main motor, and start up an engine giving directional thrust... Once the rocket has turned round, the exhaust from our nuclear motor will brake our descent. If all goes well, this will allow us to land quite gently on the Moon... You follow me?...
In fact, if I understand you correctly, it's the same procedure as for launching, but exactly the other way round.
Earth to Moon-Rocket... Stand by... Two minutes to go before stopping the main motor...
Get ready, everybody... And Captain, unless you want to start flapping about like a butterfly when the motor stops, hurry and put on your magnetic boots.
Oh Columbus! And my boots are down below!... Quick, I'll put them on...
One minute to go...
Thirty seconds to go...
Twenty seconds to go...
Ten seconds to go... Nine ... eight... seven... six... five... four... three... two... one... ZERO
I say, Captain!... Did you have time to get your boots on?
Just... I've only got to do them up...
?

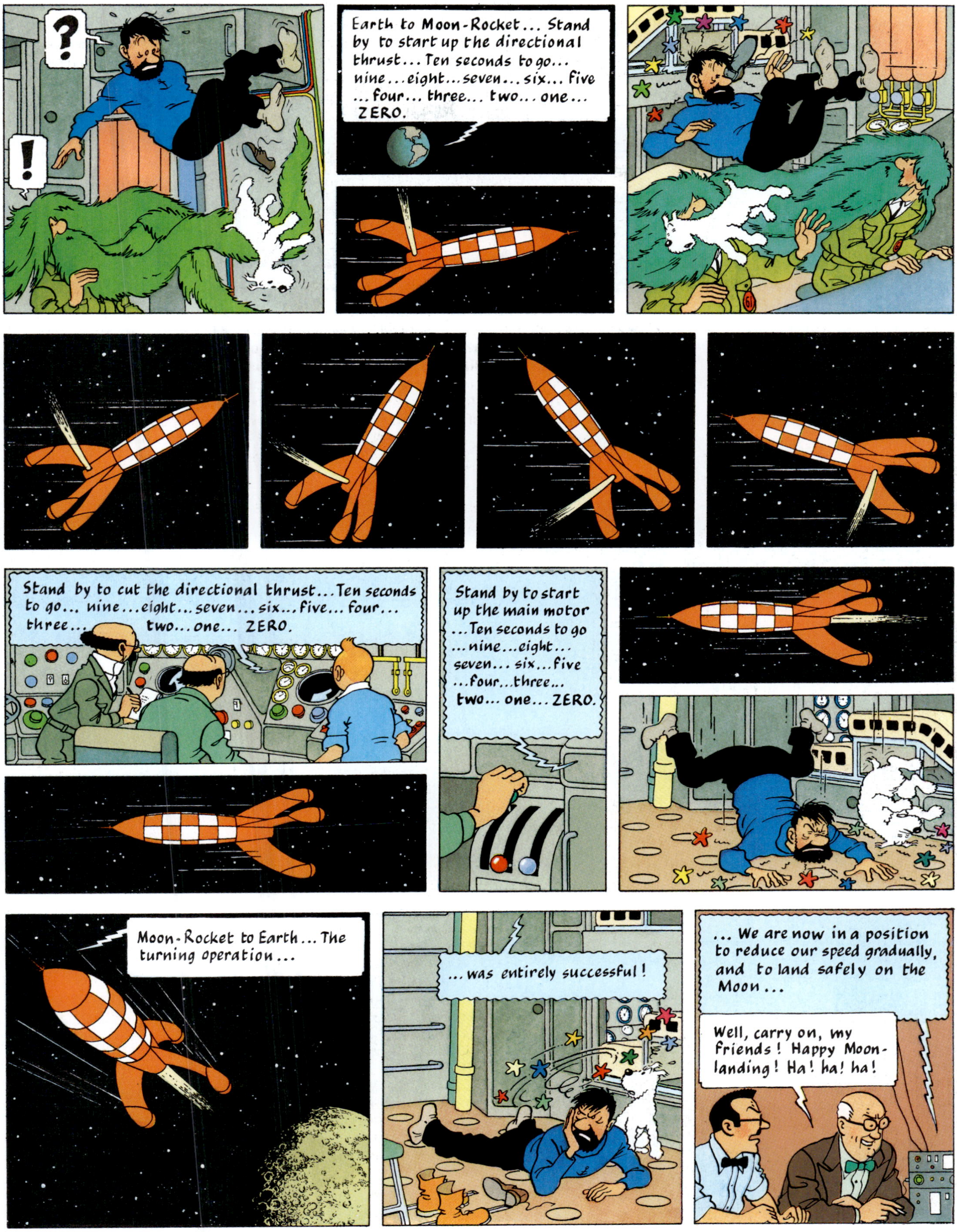
?
!
Earth to Moon-Rocket... Stand by to start up the directional thrust... Ten seconds to go... nine... eight... seven... six... five ... four... three... two... one... ZERO.
Stand by to cut the directional thrust... Ten seconds to go... nine... eight... seven... six... five... four... three... two... one... ZERO.
Stand by to start up the main motor ... Ten seconds to go ... nine... eight... seven... six... five ... four... three... two... one... ZERO.
Moon-Rocket to Earth... The turning operation...
... was entirely successful!
... We are now in a position to reduce our speed gradually, and to land safely on the Moon...
Well, carry on, my friends! Happy Moon-landing! Ha! ha! ha!

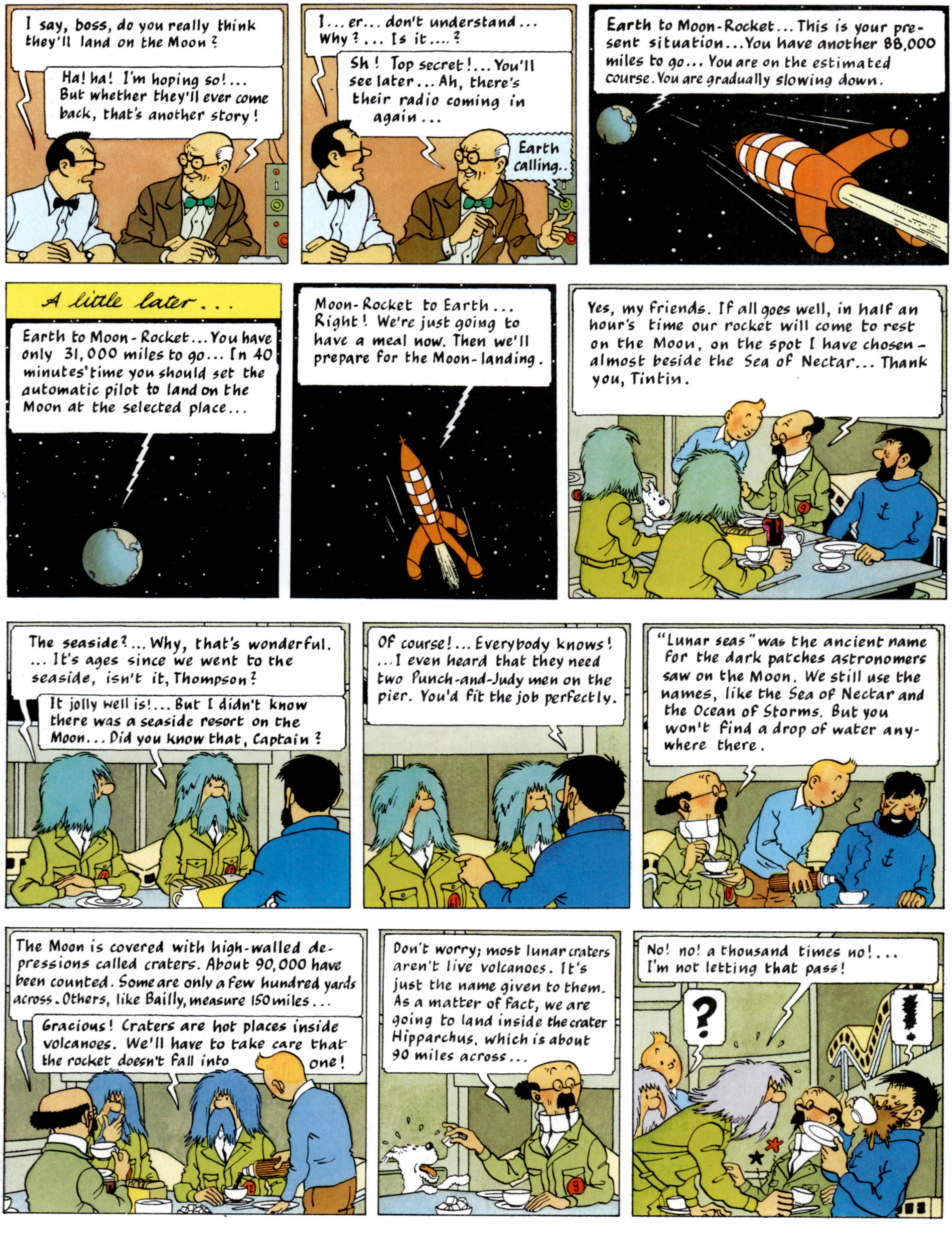
I say, boss, do you really think they'll land on the Moon ?
Ha! ha! I'm hoping so!... But whether they'll ever come back, that's another story!
I... er... don't understand... Why?... Is it....?
Sh! Top secret!... You'll see later... Ah, there's their radio coming in again...
Earth calling..
Earth to Moon-Rocket... This is your present situation... You have another 88,000 miles to go... You are on the estimated course. You are gradually slowing down.
A little later...
Earth to Moon-Rocket... You have only 31,000 miles to go... In 40 minutes' time you should set the automatic pilot to land on the Moon at the selected place...
Moon-Rocket to Earth... Right! We're just going to have a meal now. Then we'll prepare for the Moon-landing.
Yes, my friends. If all goes well, in half an hour's time our rocket will come to rest on the Moon, on the spot I have chosen - almost beside the Sea of Nectar... Thank you, Tintin.
The seaside?... Why, that's wonderful. ... It's ages since we went to the seaside, isn't it, Thompson?
It jolly well is!... But I didn't know there was a seaside resort on the Moon... Did you know that, Captain?
Of course!... Everybody knows! ...I even heard that they need two Punch-and-Judy men on the pier. You'd fit the job perfectly.
"Lunar seas" was the ancient name for the dark patches astronomers saw on the Moon. We still use the names, like the Sea of Nectar and the Ocean of Storms. But you won't find a drop of water anywhere there.
The Moon is covered with high-walled depressions called craters. About 90,000 have been counted. Some are only a few hundred yards across. Others, like Bailly, measure 150 miles...
Gracious! Craters are hot places inside volcanoes. We'll have to take care that the rocket doesn't fall into one!
Don't worry; most lunar craters aren't live volcanoes. It's just the name given to them. As a matter of fact, we are going to land inside the crater Hipparchus, which is about 90 miles across...
No! no! a thousand times no!... I'm not letting that pass!
?
!

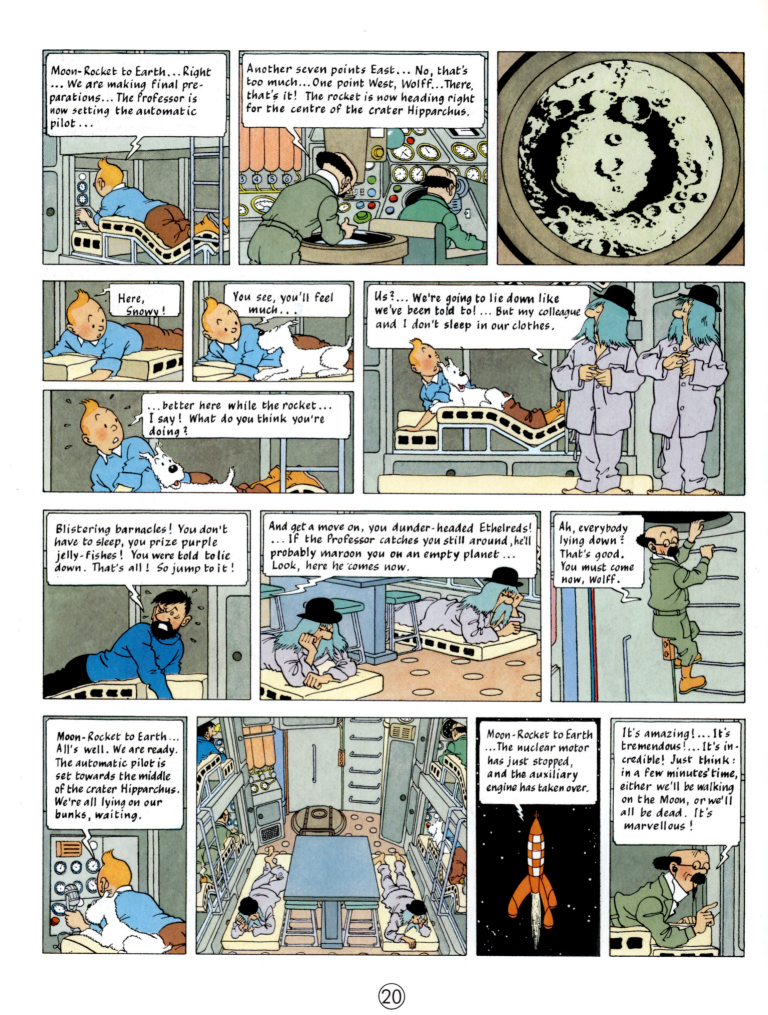

Moon-Rocket to Earth... Right ... We are making final preparations... The professor is now setting the automatic pilot...

Another seven points East... No, that's too much... One point West, Wolff... There, that's it! The rocket is now heading right for the centre of the crater Hipparchus.

Here, Snowy!

You see, you'll feel much...

...better here while the rocket... I say! What do you think you're doing?

Us?... We're going to lie down like we've been told to! ... But my colleague and I don't sleep in our clothes.

Blistering barnacles! You don't have to sleep, you prize purple jelly-fishes! You were told to lie down. That's all! So jump to it!

And get a move on, you dunder-headed Ethelreds! ...If the Professor catches you still around, he'll probably maroon you on an empty planet... Look, here he comes now.

Ah, everybody lying down? That's good. You must come now, Wolff.

Moon-Rocket to Earth... All's well. We are ready. The automatic pilot is set towards the middle of the crater Hipparchus. We're all lying on our bunks, waiting.

Moon-Rocket to Earth ...The nuclear motor has just stopped, and the auxiliary engine has taken over.

It's amazing!...It's tremendous!...It's incredible! Just think: in a few minutes' time, either we'll be walking on the Moon, or we'll all be dead. It's marvellous!

Moon-Rocket to Earth...Tintin calling...We are beginning to feel the effects of slackening speed...

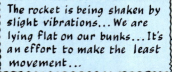
The rocket is being shaken by slight vibrations...We are lying flat on our bunks...It's an effort to make the least movement...

Our ears are ringing...The vibrations are getting stronger and stronger...The crushing sensation is worse...It's getting difficult to breathe

We're being crushed into our bunks...by an intolerable...weight ...can't move now... The Professor...blacked out ...I...think... ...I think...

...my head...will...burst! ... My eyes...I... I'm sure ... they'll pop...out of their ...sockets... I... My heart ... Oh, my heart ...

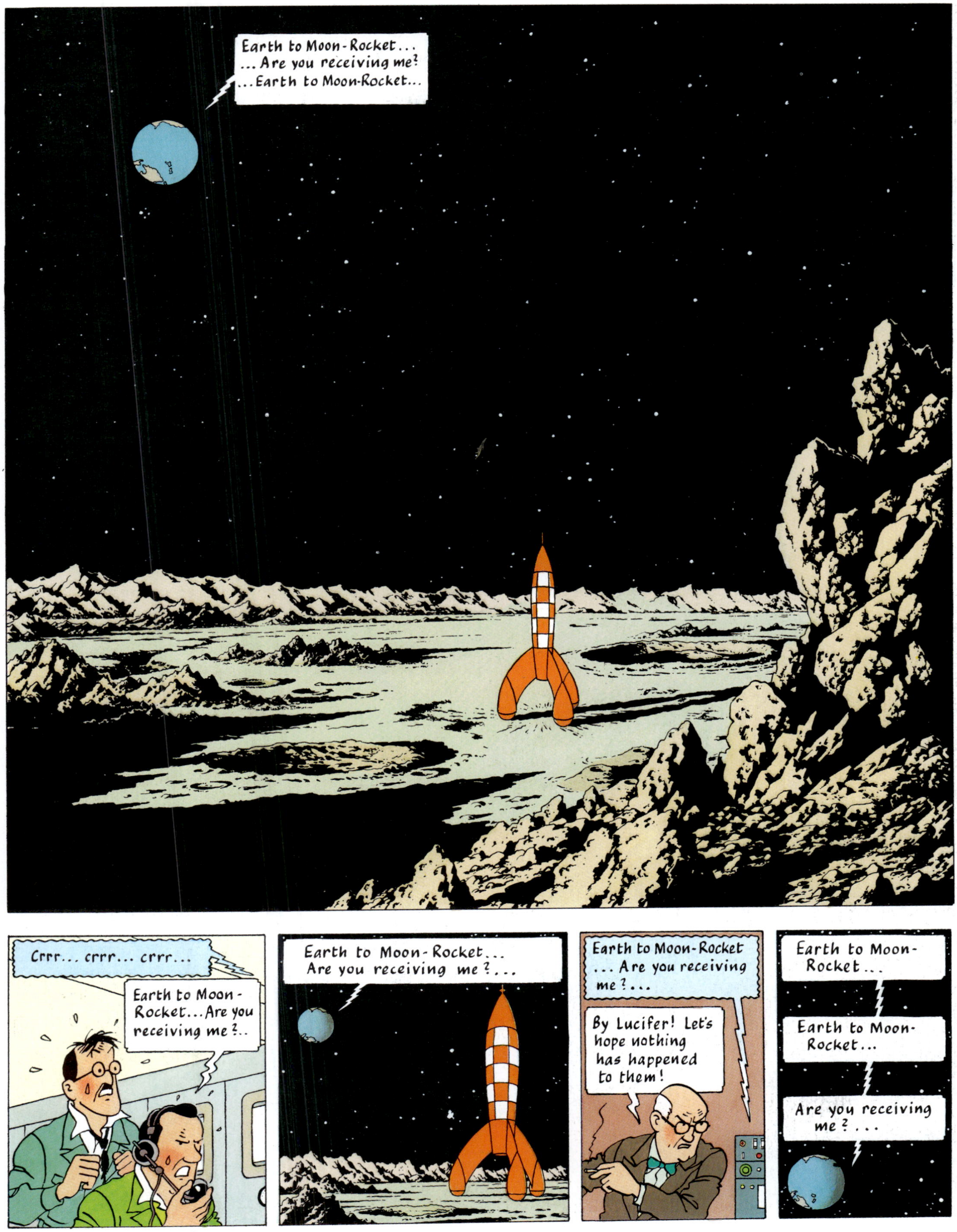
Earth to Moon-Rocket...
...Are you receiving me?
...Earth to Moon-Rocket...
Crrr... crrr... crrr...
Earth to Moon-Rocket...Are you receiving me?..
Earth to Moon-Rocket...
Are you receiving me?...
Earth to Moon-Rocket
...Are you receiving me?...
By Lucifer! Let's hope nothing has happened to them!
Earth to Moon-Rocket...
Earth to Moon-Rocket...
Are you receiving me?...

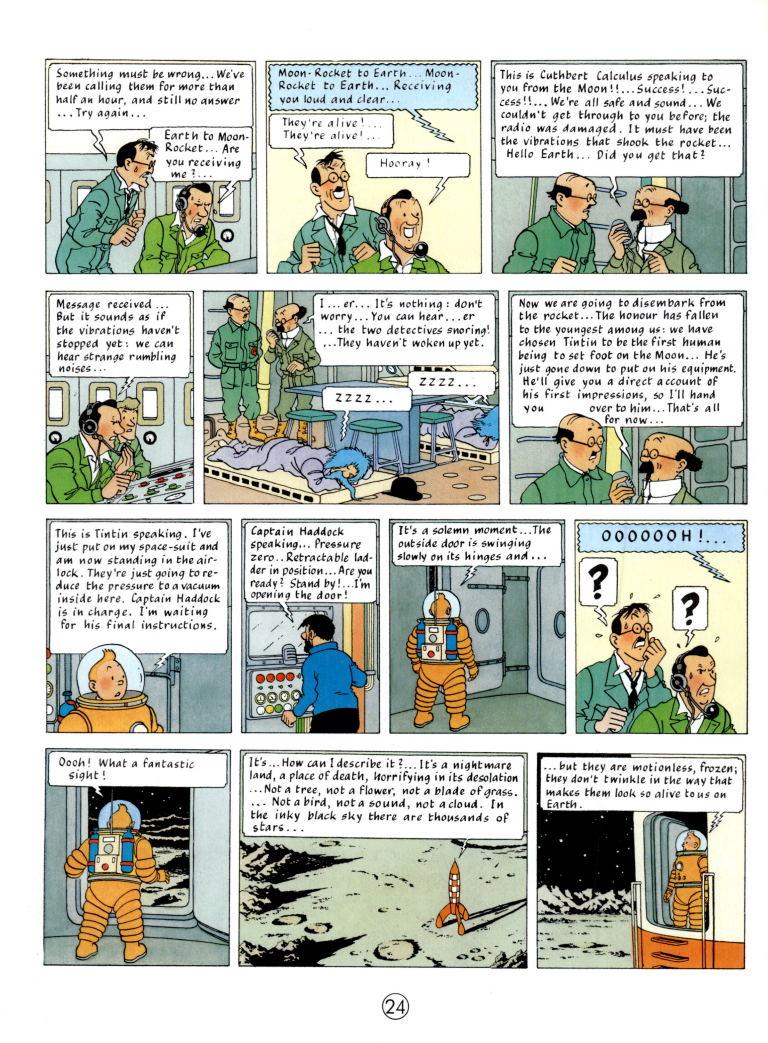

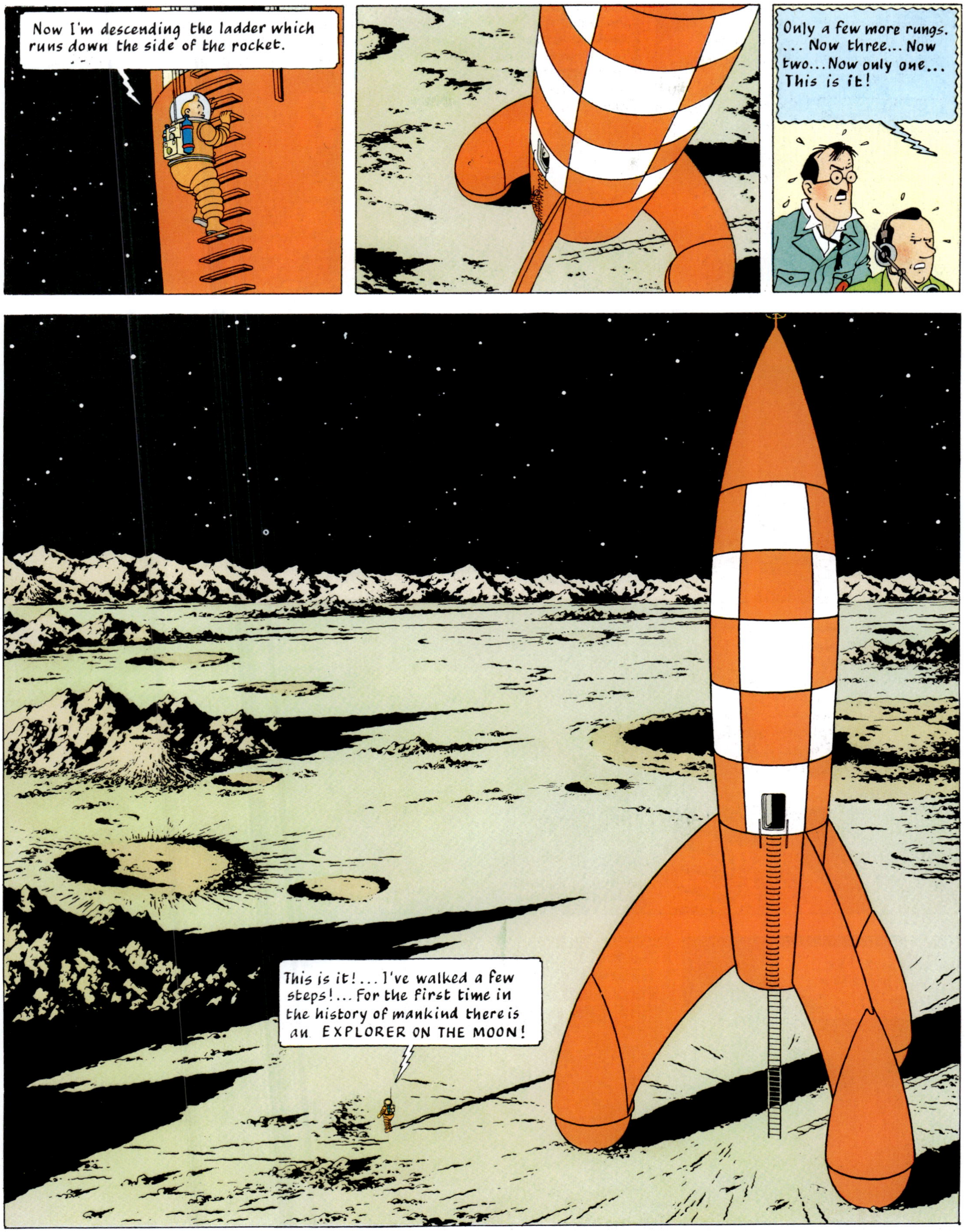
Now I'm descending the ladder which runs down the side of the rocket.
Only a few more rungs. ... Now three... Now two... Now only one... This is it!
This is it!... I've walked a few steps!... For the first time in the history of mankind there is an EXPLORER ON THE MOON!

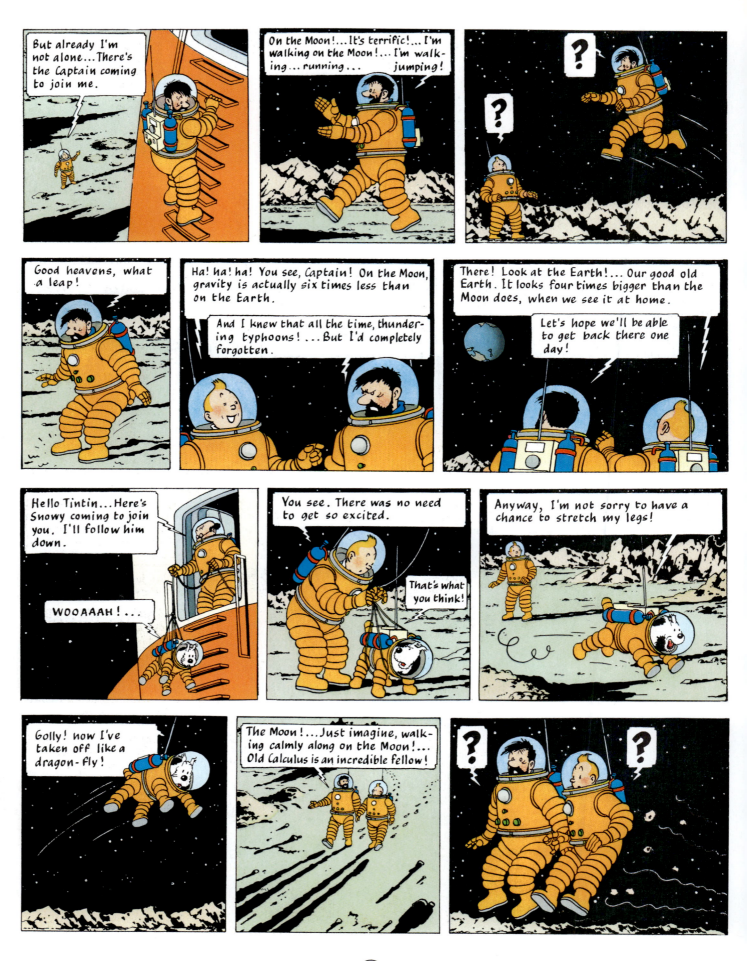

Panel 1:
What happened?... Was that an earthquake?

A Moon-quake, more likely, but...

Panel 2:
Great snakes!...Look there!

Thundering typhoons! What in the world's that?...

Panel 3:
A meteorite! Look, a meteorite! It's just fallen on the exact spot where we were a moment ago...and exploded!

Exploded? But I didn't hear a sound!

Panel 4:
Naturally not. There's no air on the Moon, so there's no noise...And that's why the meteorite came down intact, too. Back at home, on the Earth, the friction of the atmosphere would have made it white hot. So it would have disintegrated before reaching the ground, making what we generally call a "shooting star".

Panel 5:
Anyway, if those tycoons on the lunar development corporation imagine that this sort of welcome will attract tourists to the Moon, they'll have to think again.

Panel 6:
Ah, hello my friends!...This is incredible!... It's fantastic!...We're on the Moon! D'you realise that?

Oh, so there you are!

Panel 7:
Just take a look there!... A little bit closer, and you'd have been able to throw away our return tickets!.

A meteorite! How marvellous!

Panel 8:
Oh, so you think that's marvellous, do you? When we'd have been as flat as pancakes!

What do you expect? It's an occupational hazard!

Panel 9:
Exactly, blistering barnacles! But this isn't my occupation! Thundering typhoons, I'm a sailor!...And on board ship, at least you don't run the risk of bits of sky falling down all over the place, every time you bat an eyelid!

Maybe!...But just try coming to the Moon by boat!

Panel 10:
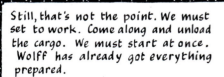

Still, that's not the point. We must set to work. Come along and unload the cargo. We must start at once. Wolff has already got everything prepared.

Panel 11:
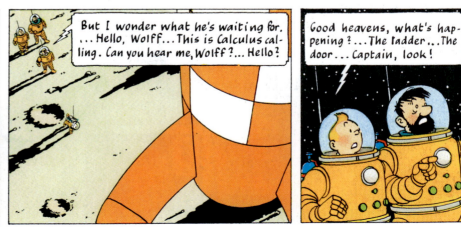
But I wonder what he's waiting for. ...Hello, Wolff...This is Calculus calling. Can you hear me, Wolff?... Hello?

Panel 12:

Good heavens, what's happening?...The ladder...The door...Captain, look!

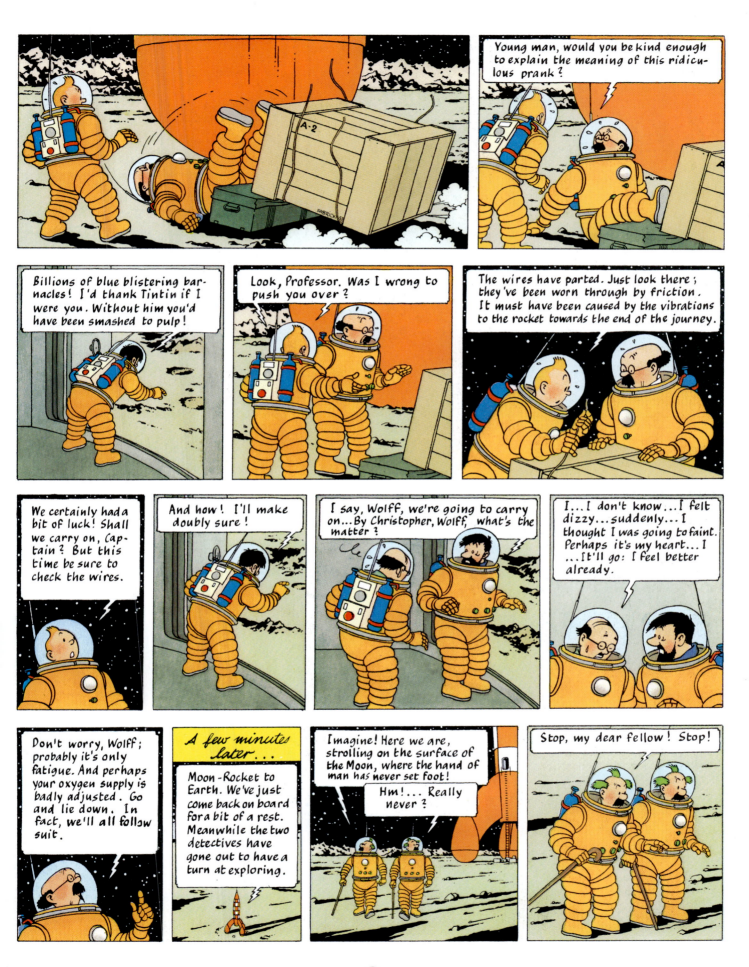

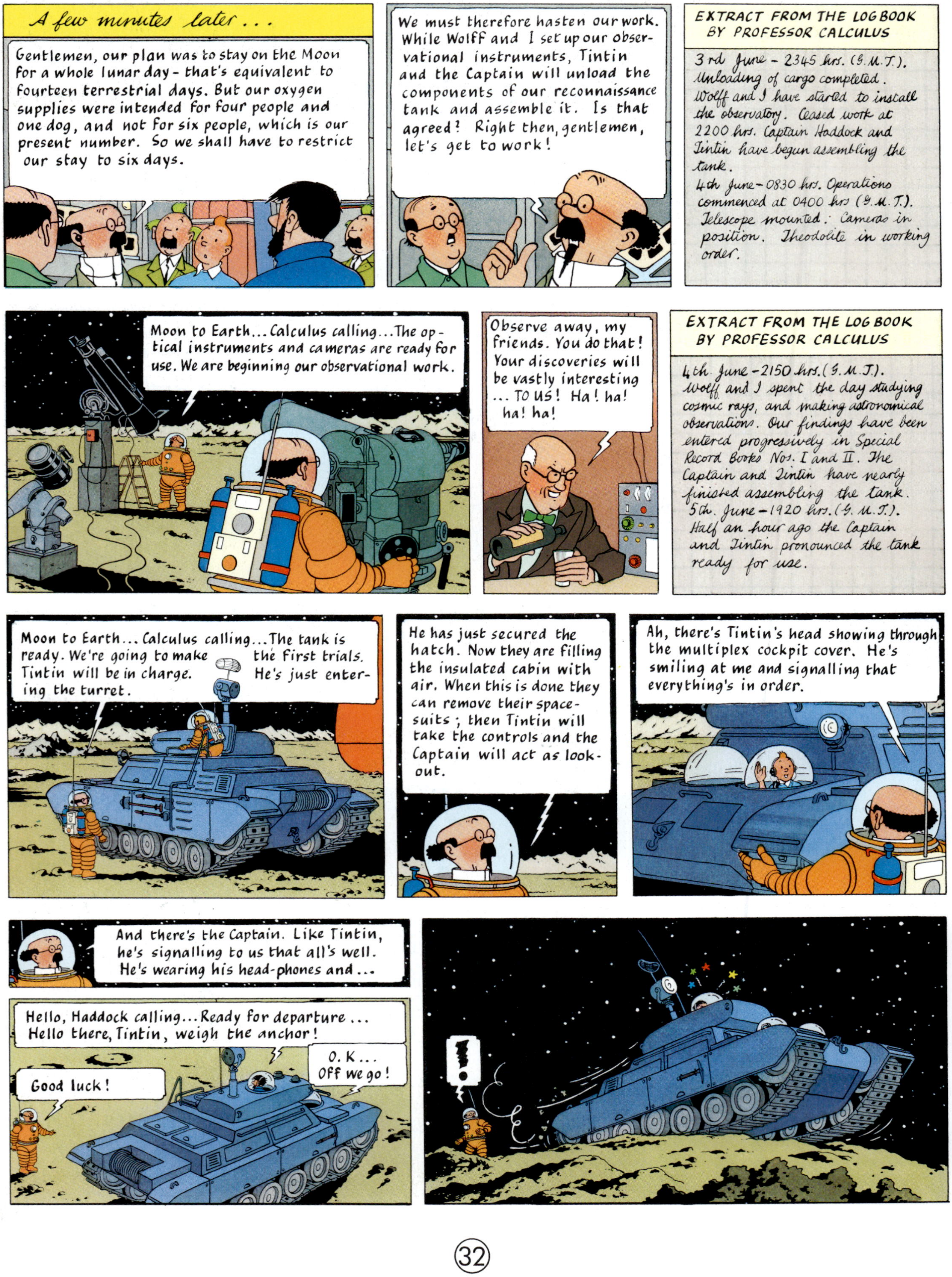
A few minutes later . . .
Gentlemen, our plan was to stay on the Moon for a whole lunar day - that's equivalent to fourteen terrestrial days. But our oxygen supplies were intended for four people and one dog, and not for six people, which is our present number. So we shall have to restrict our stay to six days.
We must therefore hasten our work. While Wolff and I set up our observational instruments, Tintin and the Captain will unload the components of our reconnaissance tank and assemble it. Is that agreed? Right then, gentlemen, let's get to work!
EXTRACT FROM THE LOG BOOK BY PROFESSOR CALCULUS
3rd June - 2345 hrs. (G. M. T.). Unloading of cargo completed. Wolff and I have started to install the observatory. Ceased work at 2200 hrs. Captain Haddock and Tintin have begun assembling the tank.
4th June - 0830 hrs. Operations commenced at 0400 hrs (G. M. T.). Telescope mounted: Cameras in position. Theodolite in working order.
Moon to Earth... Calculus calling... The optical instruments and cameras are ready for use. We are beginning our observational work.
Observe away, my friends. You do that! Your discoveries will be vastly interesting ... TO US! Ha! ha! ha! ha!
EXTRACT FROM THE LOG BOOK BY PROFESSOR CALCULUS
4th June - 2150 hrs. (G. M. T.). Wolff and I spent the day studying cosmic rays, and making astronomical observations. Our findings have been entered progressively in Special Record Books Nos. I and II. The Captain and Tintin have nearly finished assembling the tank.
5th. June - 1920 hrs. (G. M. T.). Half an hour ago the Captain and Tintin pronounced the tank ready for use.
Moon to Earth... Calculus calling... The tank is ready. We're going to make the first trials. Tintin will be in charge. He's just entering the turret.
He has just secured the hatch. Now they are filling the insulated cabin with air. When this is done they can remove their space-suits; then Tintin will take the controls and the Captain will act as look-out.
Ah, there's Tintin's head showing through the multiplex cockpit cover. He's smiling at me and signalling that everything's in order.
And there's the Captain. Like Tintin, he's signalling to us that all's well. He's wearing his head-phones and ...
Hello, Haddock calling... Ready for departure ... Hello there, Tintin, weigh the anchor!
O. K ... Off we go!
Good luck!
!!!

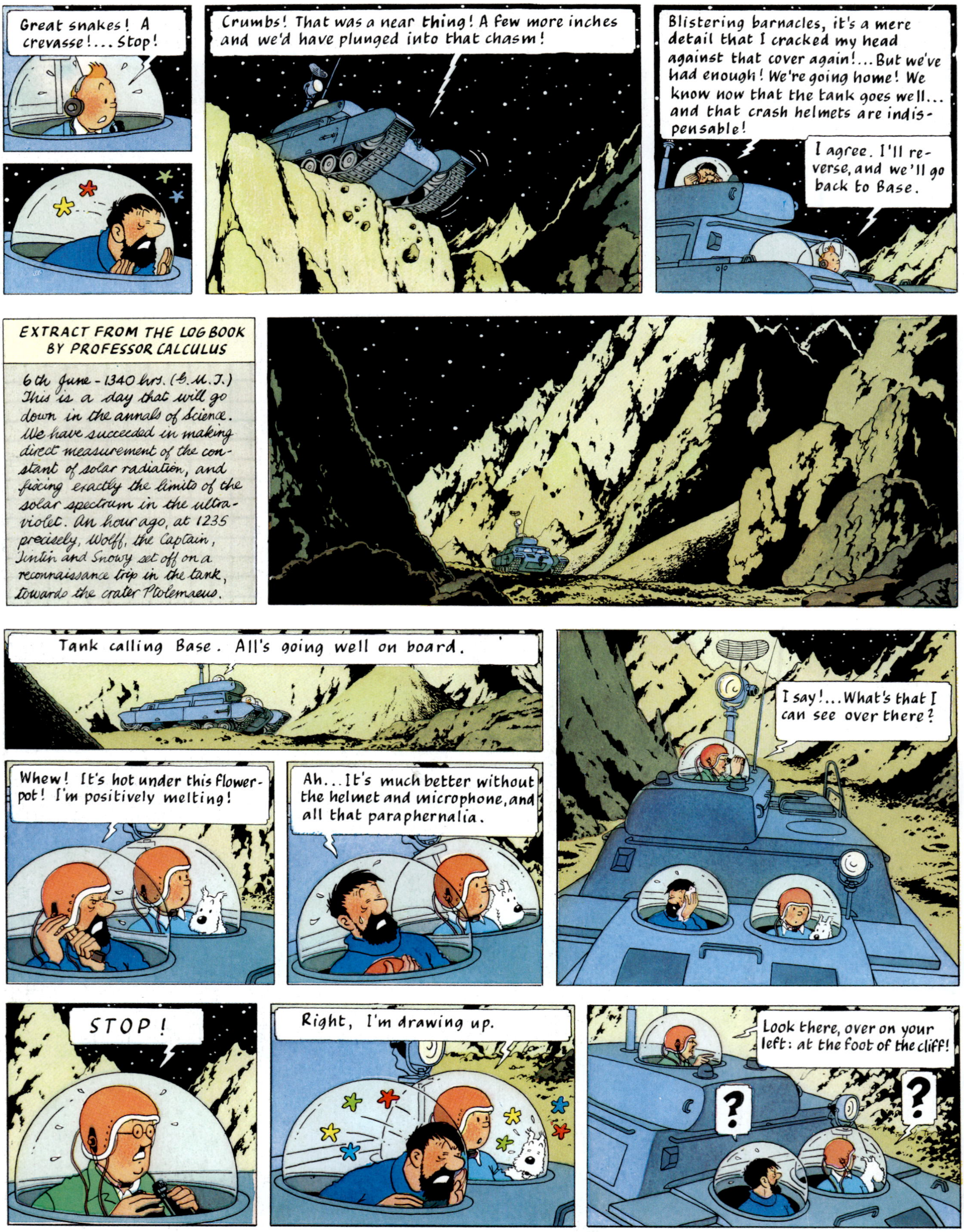
Great snakes! A crevasse!... Stop!
Crumbs! That was a near thing! A few more inches and we'd have plunged into that chasm!
Blistering barnacles, it's a mere detail that I cracked my head against that cover again!... But we've had enough! We're going home! We know now that the tank goes well... and that crash helmets are indispensable!
I agree. I'll reverse, and we'll go back to Base.
EXTRACT FROM THE LOG BOOK BY PROFESSOR CALCULUS
6th June - 1340 hrs. (G.M.T.) This is a day that will go down in the annals of Science. We have succeeded in making direct measurement of the constant of solar radiation, and fixing exactly the limits of the solar spectrum in the ultra-violet. An hour ago, at 1235 precisely, Wolff, the Captain, Tintin and Snowy set off on a reconnaissance trip in the tank, towards the crater Ptolemaeus.
Tank calling Base. All's going well on board.
Whew! It's hot under this flower-pot! I'm positively melting!
Ah... It's much better without the helmet and microphone, and all that paraphernalia.
I say!... What's that I can see over there?
STOP!
Right, I'm drawing up.
Look there, over on your left: at the foot of the cliff!
?
?

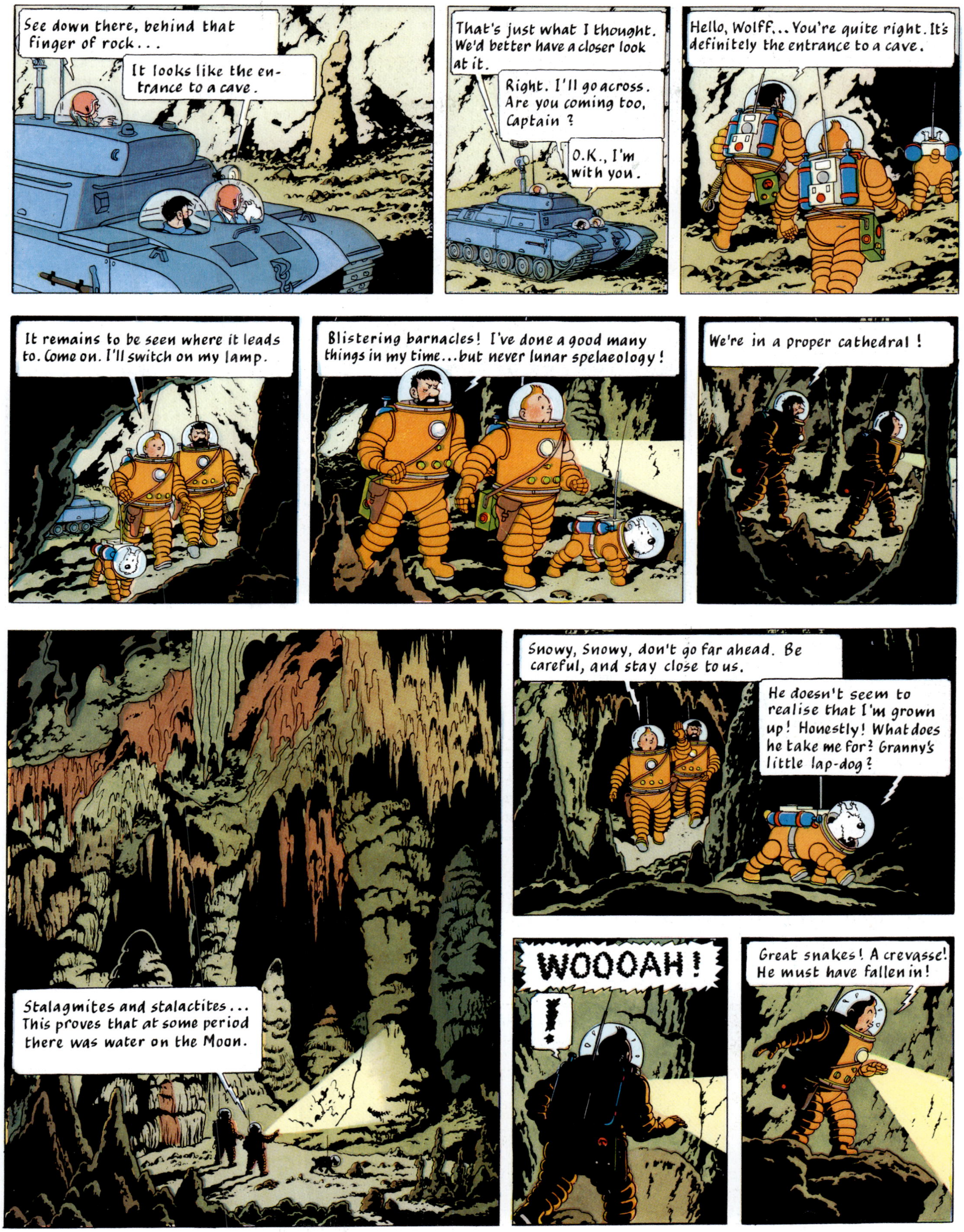
See down there, behind that finger of rock...
It looks like the entrance to a cave.
That's just what I thought. We'd better have a closer look at it.
Right. I'll go across. Are you coming too, Captain ?
O.K., I'm with you.
Hello, Wolff... You're quite right. It's definitely the entrance to a cave.
It remains to be seen where it leads to. Come on. I'll switch on my lamp.
Blistering barnacles! I've done a good many things in my time... but never lunar spelaeology!
We're in a proper cathedral!
Stalagmites and stalactites... This proves that at some period there was water on the Moon.
Snowy, Snowy, don't go far ahead. Be careful, and stay close to us.
He doesn't seem to realise that I'm grown up! Honestly! What does he take me for? Granny's little lap-dog?
WOOOAH!
!
Great snakes! A crevasse! He must have fallen in!

Snowy!... You're there! Nothing broken? But what's the matter? You aren't answering... Oh, now I see: your radio isn't working.

Hello, Captain... I've found Snowy! He's safe and sound. But his radio's smashed. I'll climb back up to the rope.

My dear Tintin, you don't imagine you can stand up on this skating-rink, do you?

You see? What did I tell you?

Crumbs! How can I climb this icy slope?... There's only one way to do it: by cutting steps with a chunk of rock. Oh well, to work!

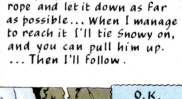
Hello, Captain... Untie the rope and let it down as far as possible... When I manage to reach it I'll tie Snowy on, and you can pull him up. ... Then I'll follow.

O.K.

Here we are at last!

Hello, Captain. Let out more rope: it isn't down far enough for me to tie it round Snowy.

Right.

That's done it.

A few minutes later...

Hello Tintin... That's it... Snowy is safe now.

Hello Tintin... I've secured a heavy stone to the end of the rope. I'm letting it down...

All right, Captain. But hurry: it's beginning to get difficult to breathe.

I'm almost at the end. Can you see the rope?

No, I can't see it. Do please hurry!

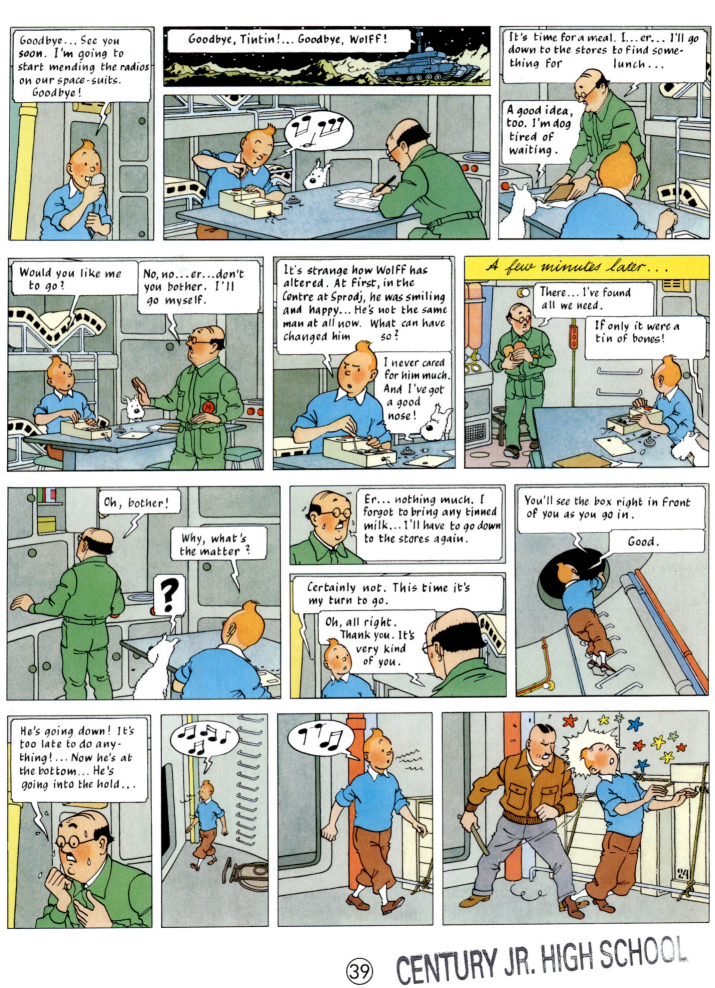

CENTURY JR. HIGH SCHOOL

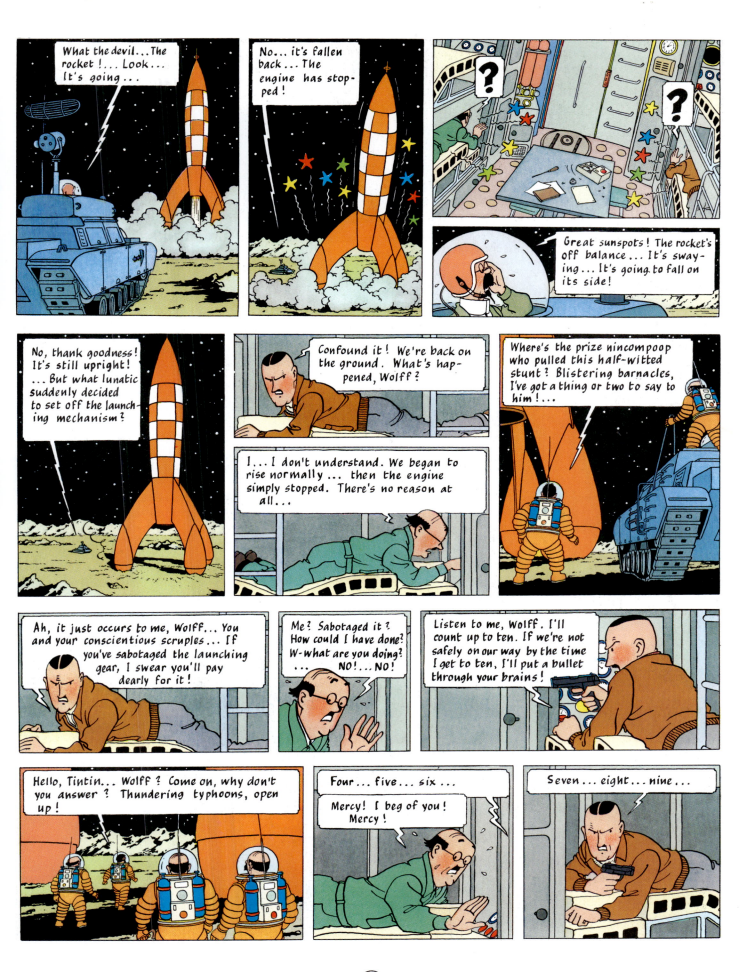

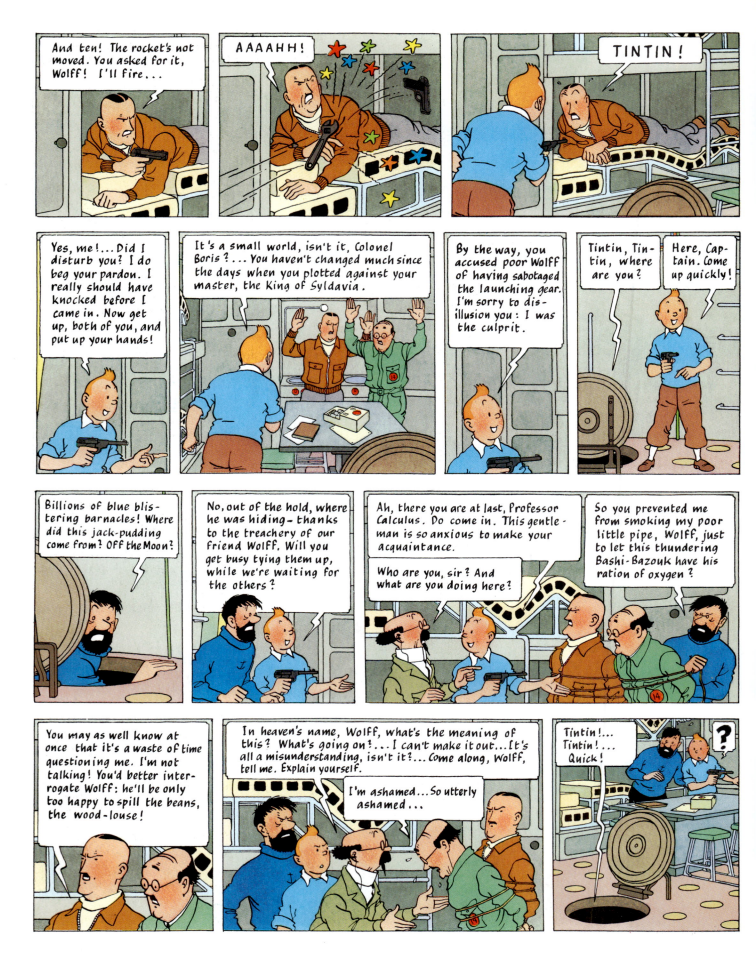

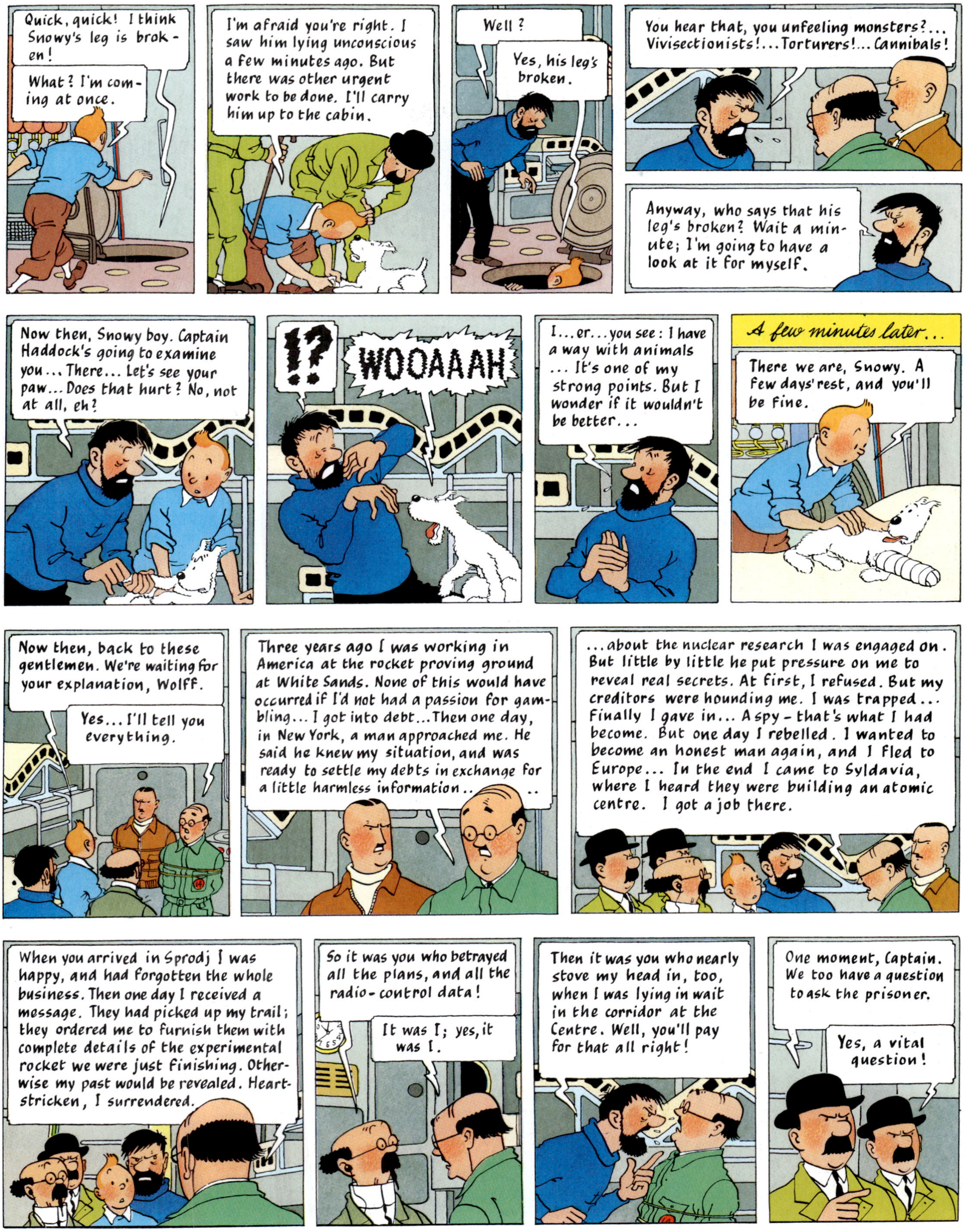

Quick, quick! I think Snowy's leg is brok-en!
What? I'm com-ing at once.
I'm afraid you're right. I saw him lying unconscious a few minutes ago. But there was other urgent work to be done. I'll carry him up to the cabin.
Well?
Yes, his leg's broken.
You hear that, you unfeeling monsters?... Vivisectionists!... Torturers!... Cannibals!
Anyway, who says that his leg's broken? Wait a min-ute; I'm going to have a look at it for myself.
Now then, Snowy boy. Captain Haddock's going to examine you... There... Let's see your paw... Does that hurt? No, not at all, eh?
!?
WOOAAAH
I...er...you see: I have a way with animals ... It's one of my strong points. But I wonder if it wouldn't be better...
A few minutes later...
There we are, Snowy. A few days' rest, and you'll be fine.
Now then, back to these gentlemen. We're waiting for your explanation, Wolff.
Yes... I'll tell you everything.
Three years ago I was working in America at the rocket proving ground at White Sands. None of this would have occurred if I'd not had a passion for gam-bling... I got into debt... Then one day, in New York, a man approached me. He said he knew my situation, and was ready to settle my debts in exchange for a little harmless information...
...about the nuclear research I was engaged on. But little by little he put pressure on me to reveal real secrets. At first, I refused. But my creditors were hounding me. I was trapped... Finally I gave in... A spy - that's what I had become. But one day I rebelled. I wanted to become an honest man again, and I fled to Europe... In the end I came to Syldavia, where I heard they were building an atomic centre. I got a job there.
When you arrived in Sprodj I was happy, and had forgotten the whole business. Then one day I received a message. They had picked up my trail; they ordered me to furnish them with complete details of the experimental rocket we were just finishing. Other-wise my past would be revealed. Heart-stricken, I surrendered.
So it was you who betrayed all the plans, and all the radio-control data!
It was I; yes, it was I.
Then it was you who nearly stove my head in, too, when I was lying in wait in the corridor at the Centre. Well, you'll pay for that all right!
One moment, Captain. We too have a question to ask the prisoner.
Yes, a vital question!

Undoubtedly by cutting the leads Tintin averted disaster...for the time being. Alas, it is only too likely that in falling, the rocket suffered serious damage. And this will probably take time to repair. Meanwhile, there's still the grave problem of the oxygen...But let's hear the rest of your story, Tintin.

Where was I?...Oh yes. Once the rocket grounded, I opened the door of the air-lock and lowered the retractable ladder, so that you could get in. Then, having armed myself with a pistol and spanner, I came quietly up to the cabin... I found myself right in the middle of a family squabble...

This thug accused Wolff of sabotaging the launching gear, and was going to shoot him. My spanner knocked his gun out of his hand. Just in time, wasn't it, my dear Jorgen...as it seems that you are no longer Colonel Boris.

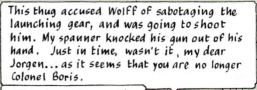

Why, do you know this pithecanthropus?

Oh yes, we met in Syldavia, over that business of King Ottokar's Sceptre. Under the name of Boris, he was aide-de-camp to King Muskar XII, whom he shamefully betrayed. I won the first round, but for a while he seemed to be winning the second...

And now we'll dump these two down in the hold.

What?...While we risk running out of oxygen, we're going to clutter the place up with these pirates? They were going to abandon us on the Moon: well, that's the fate they deserve themselves, by thunder!

We must be more chivalrous than they were, Captain... Now, you're the expert, so take them below and tie them up securely.

As you like! But you'll live to regret your noble gesture. Mark my words: you'll regret it!

Anyway, my little lambs, I'm going to knit you lovely little rope waistcoats to keep you nice and warm! Hand-made, by thunder! Guaranteed absolutely perfect!

Do what you like with me. But please be kind enough to stop spluttering in my face- it's wet!

What?...Me?...Wet?...Blistering barnacles, you dare... A man of spirit like me! To hear myself insulted, by this creature, this Bashi-bazouk!

Calm down, Captain, calm down!

Calm down? Calm down?...But you heard him, this little black-beetle! Daring to make out that I'm wet! Calm down! I like that, from you!

To call me wet!... What a nerve!

Calculus has got one.

Yes, I'll fetch it

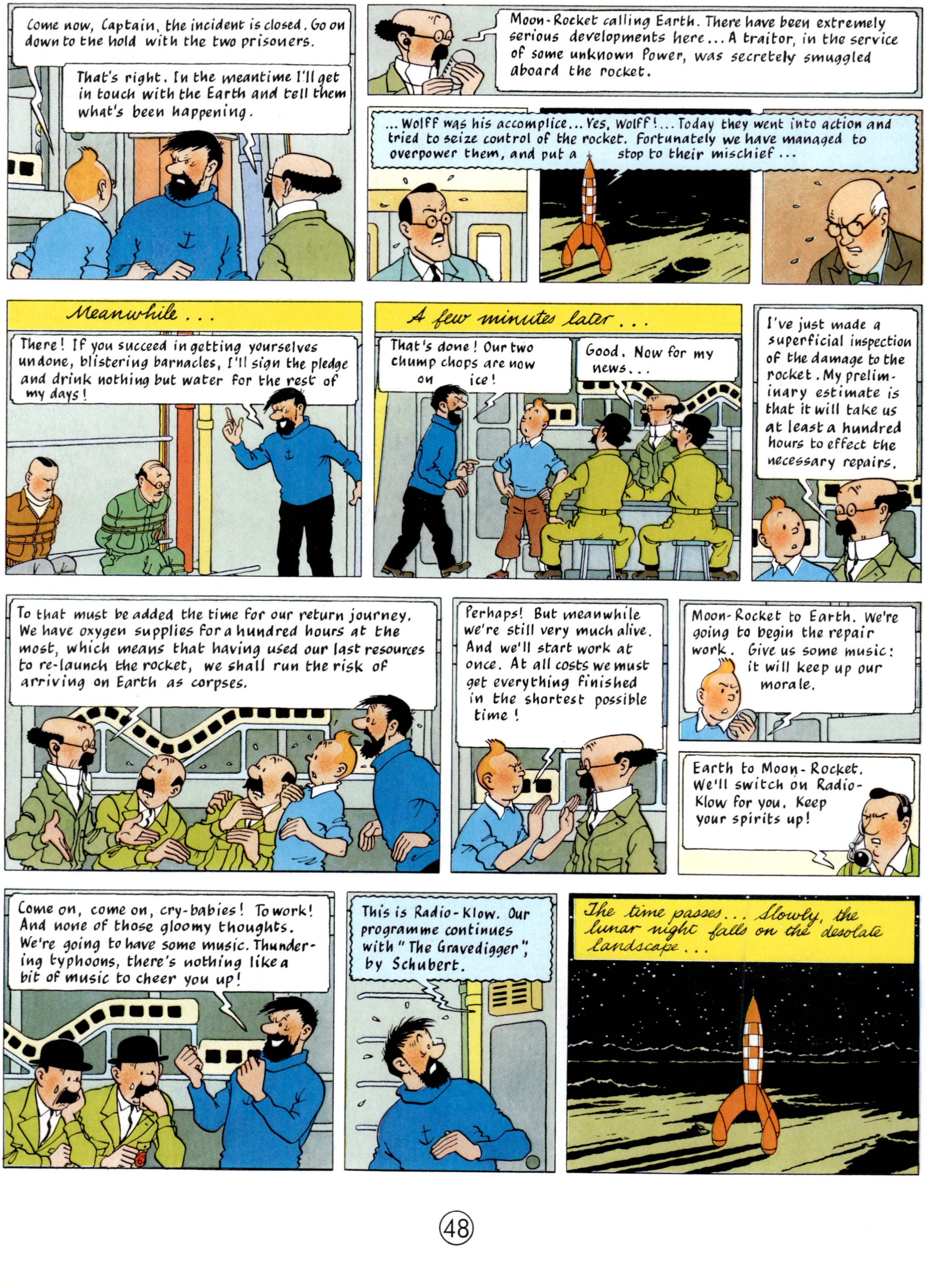
Come now, Captain, the incident is closed. Go on down to the hold with the two prisoners.
That's right. In the meantime I'll get in touch with the Earth and tell them what's been happening.
Moon-Rocket calling Earth. There have been extremely serious developments here... A traitor, in the service of some unknown Power, was secretely smuggled aboard the rocket.
...Wolff was his accomplice... Yes, Wolff!... Today they went into action and tried to seize control of the rocket. Fortunately we have managed to overpower them, and put a stop to their mischief...
Meanwhile...
There! If you succeed in getting yourselves undone, blistering barnacles, I'll sign the pledge and drink nothing but water for the rest of my days!
A few minutes later...
That's done! Our two chump chops are now on ice!
Good. Now for my news...
I've just made a superficial inspection of the damage to the rocket. My preliminary estimate is that it will take us at least a hundred hours to effect the necessary repairs.
To that must be added the time for our return journey. We have oxygen supplies for a hundred hours at the most, which means that having used our last resources to re-launch the rocket, we shall run the risk of arriving on Earth as corpses.
Perhaps! But meanwhile we're still very much alive. And we'll start work at once. At all costs we must get everything finished in the shortest possible time!
Moon-Rocket to Earth. We're going to begin the repair work. Give us some music: it will keep up our morale.
Earth to Moon-Rocket. We'll switch on Radio-Klow for you. Keep your spirits up!
Come on, come on, cry-babies! To work! And none of those gloomy thoughts. We're going to have some music. Thundering typhoons, there's nothing like a bit of music to cheer you up!
This is Radio-Klow. Our programme continues with "The Gravedigger", by Schubert.
The time passes... Slowly, the lunar night falls on the desolate landscape...

Seventy-two hours have gone by...

Moon-Rocket to Earth... The work is well ahead. Barring accidents, we shall have finished by midday... However, we are having to abandon the tank and the optical instruments on the Moon. To dismantle them and then reload them would take too long, in view of the little oxygen remaining.

We are only keeping the recording instruments, the cameras, and, of course, the oxygen cylinders from the tank. They constitute our final reserves. Tintin and the Captain have gone to collect them. I'm switching over now, as I want to keep in touch with them.

Right.

Hello Tintin... Calculus here... How are you getting on?

All right, thanks. But the sun has completely vanished. Only the mountain-tops are still glowing on the horizon...

But it's not preventing us from seeing, as there's a wonderful light from the Earth.

Pom Pom Pom ♩ ♪ And they danced ♪ by the ♩ light of ♩ the Earth ♩

We have left a message sealed inside the tank for those who may one day follow in our steps. If we are lost with all hands, this message will be a reminder of the fantastic adventures of the first men on the Moon. Now we are coming back on board.

A few minutes later...

Everything's in order, Professor.

Good. Well, I've finished all the repairs. Earth have just given me the result of their reckoning. Take-off should be at 1652 hours. So we have about two hours to go.

I advise you to lie down, to save oxygen. But before doing that, Captain, would you go to the hold and make the prisoners lie down as well, so that they won't suffer too much.

What?? And would you like me to take them breakfast in bed?

Keeping them is crazy enough! But to coddle them like babes in arms ... blistering barnacles, that's the limit! Still, I'll go.

Patience! I've not struck my last blow yet! But ssh! Someone's coming...

Two hours later...

Earth calling Moon-Rocket... Stand by ... Stand by...

Thirty seconds to go... Twenty seconds to go... Ten seconds to go... nine... eight... seven... six... five... four ...three... two... one... ZERO!

I press the button... and pray that everything works properly! Otherwise, we're condemned to death!

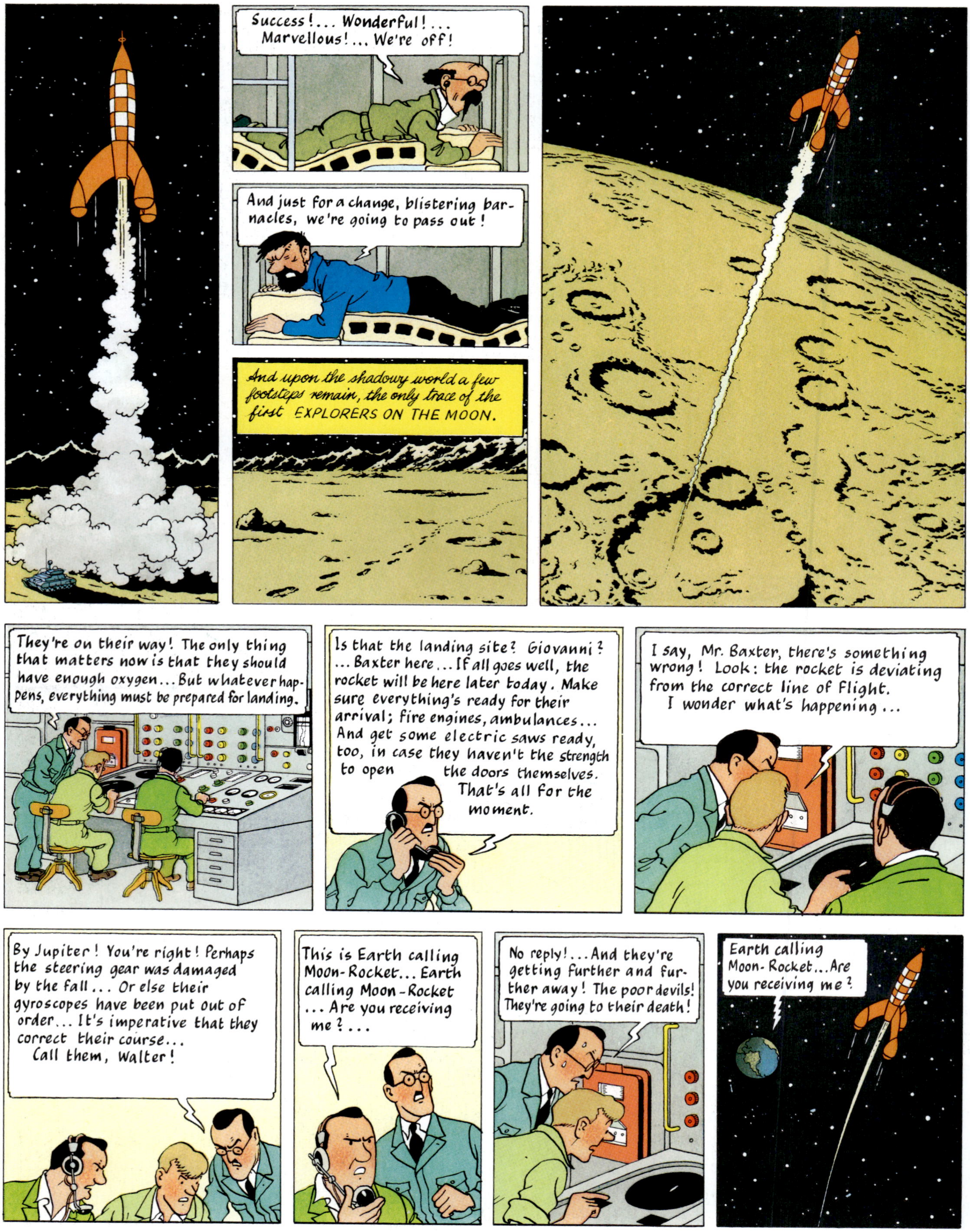

Success!... Wonderful!... Marvellous!... We're off!
And just for a change, blistering barnacles, we're going to pass out!
And upon the shadowy world a few footsteps remain, the only trace of the first EXPLORERS ON THE MOON.
They're on their way! The only thing that matters now is that they should have enough oxygen... But whatever happens, everything must be prepared for landing.
Is that the landing site? Giovanni? ... Baxter here... If all goes well, the rocket will be here later today. Make sure everything's ready for their arrival; fire engines, ambulances... And get some electric saws ready, too, in case they haven't the strength to open the doors themselves. That's all for the moment.
I say, Mr. Baxter, there's something wrong! Look: the rocket is deviating from the correct line of flight. I wonder what's happening...
By Jupiter! You're right! Perhaps the steering gear was damaged by the fall... Or else their gyroscopes have been put out of order... It's imperative that they correct their course... Call them, Walter!
This is Earth calling Moon-Rocket... Earth calling Moon-Rocket ... Are you receiving me?...
No reply!... And they're getting further and further away! The poor devils! They're going to their death!
Earth calling Moon-Rocket... Are you receiving me?

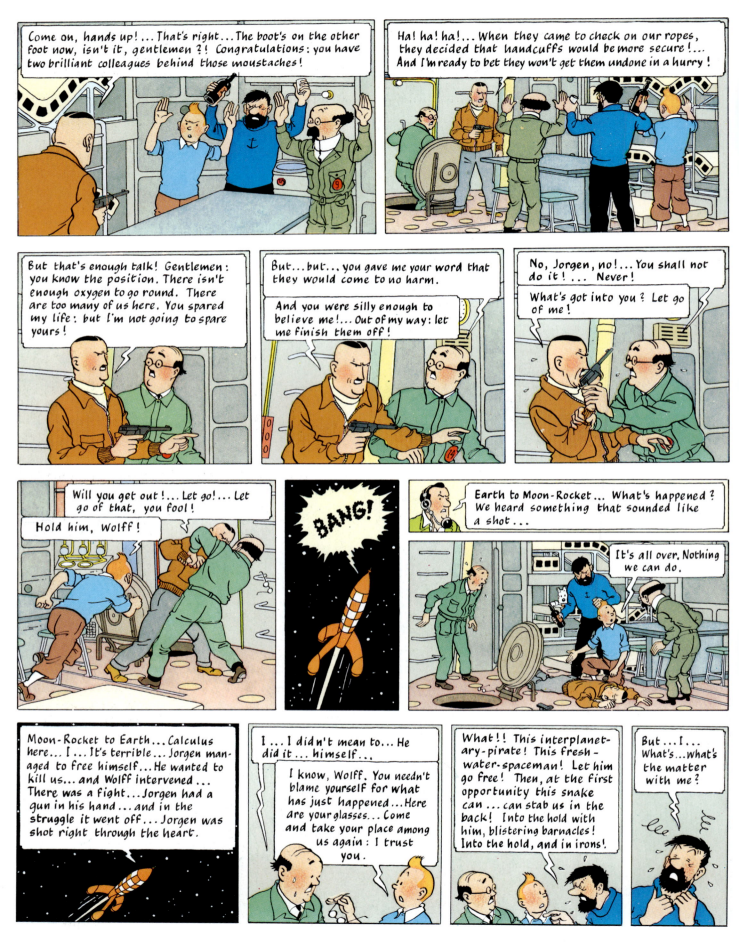

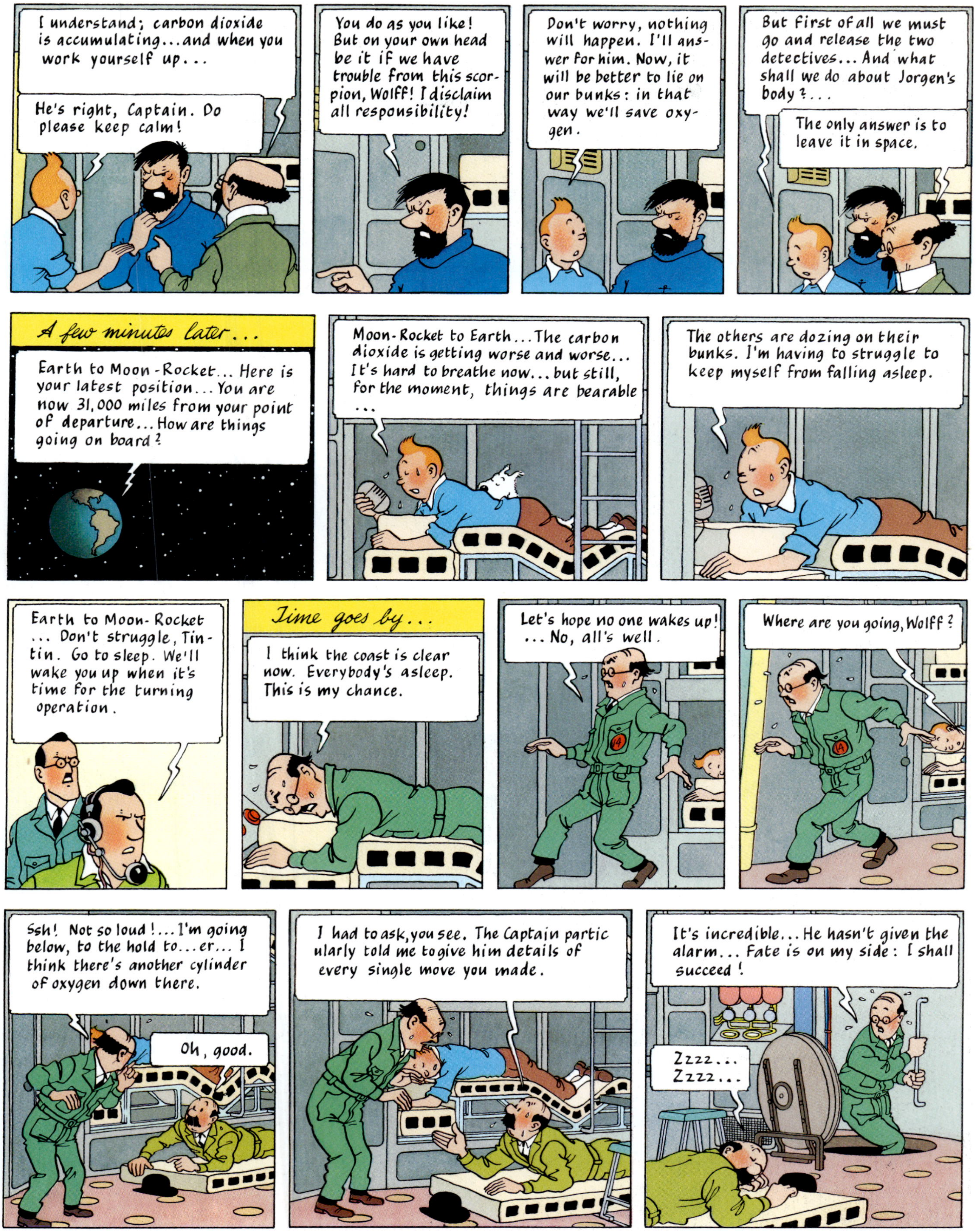
I understand; carbon dioxide is accumulating...and when you work yourself up...
He's right, Captain. Do please keep calm!
You do as you like! But on your own head be it if we have trouble from this scorpion, Wolff! I disclaim all responsibility!
Don't worry, nothing will happen. I'll answer for him. Now, it will be better to lie on our bunks: in that way we'll save oxygen.
But first of all we must go and release the two detectives... And what shall we do about Jorgen's body?...
The only answer is to leave it in space.
A few minutes later...
Earth to Moon-Rocket... Here is your latest position... You are now 31,000 miles from your point of departure... How are things going on board?
Moon-Rocket to Earth... The carbon dioxide is getting worse and worse... It's hard to breathe now... but still, for the moment, things are bearable...
The others are dozing on their bunks. I'm having to struggle to keep myself from falling asleep.
Earth to Moon-Rocket... Don't struggle, Tintin. Go to sleep. We'll wake you up when it's time for the turning operation.
Time goes by...
I think the coast is clear now. Everybody's asleep. This is my chance.
Let's hope no one wakes up! ... No, all's well.
Where are you going, Wolff?
Ssh! Not so loud!... I'm going below, to the hold to... er... I think there's another cylinder of oxygen down there.
Oh, good.
I had to ask, you see. The Captain particularly told me to give him details of every single move you made.
It's incredible... He hasn't given the alarm... Fate is on my side: I shall succeed!
Zzzz... Zzzz...

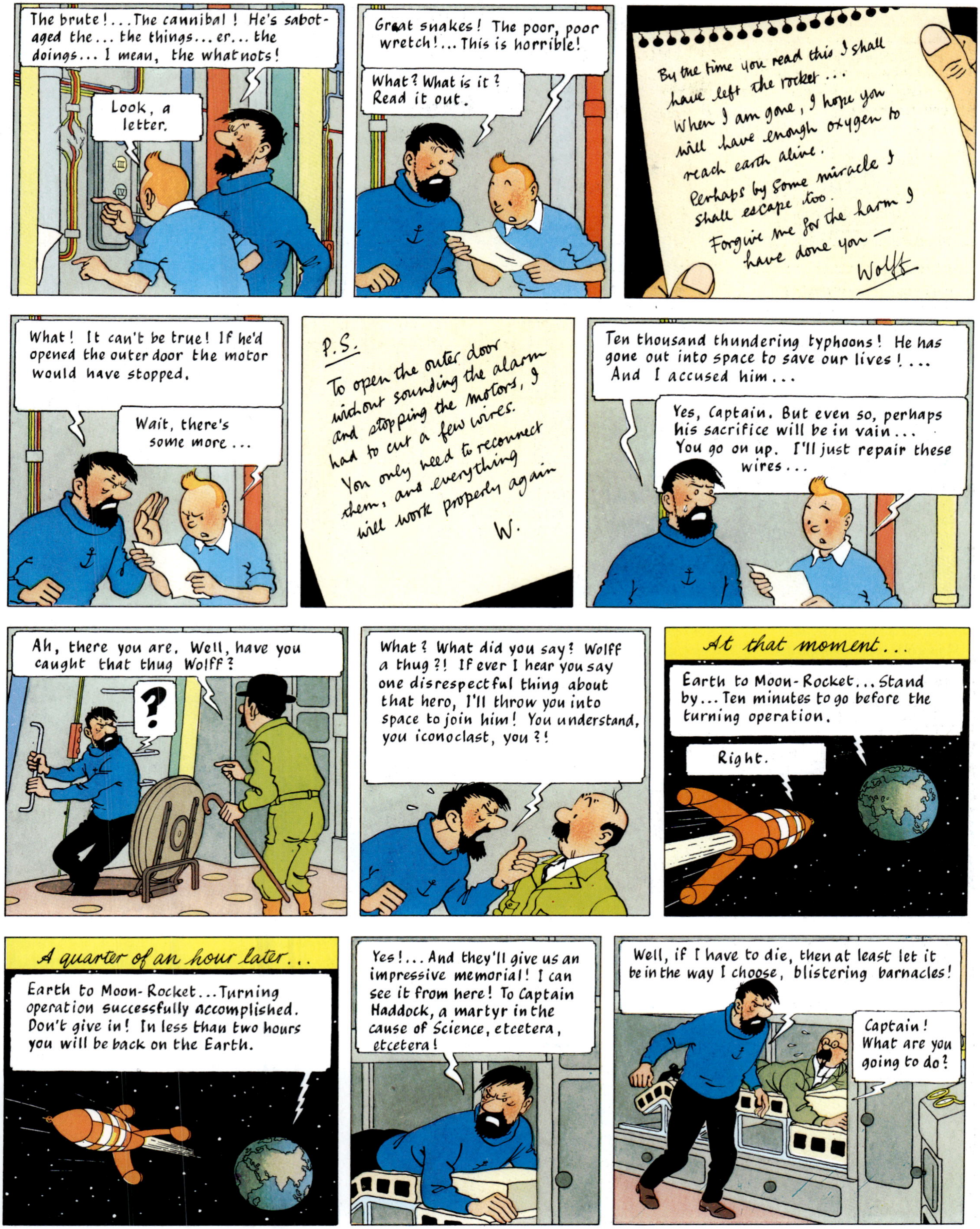

The brute!...The cannibal! He's sabotaged the... the things... er... the doings... I mean, the whatnots!
Look, a letter.
Great snakes! The poor, poor wretch!... This is horrible!
What? What is it? Read it out.
By the time you read this I shall have left the rocket... When I am gone, I hope you will have enough oxygen to reach earth alive. Perhaps by some miracle I shall escape too. Forgive me for the harm I have done you — Wolff
What! It can't be true! If he'd opened the outer door the motor would have stopped.
Wait, there's some more...
P.S. To open the outer door without sounding the alarm and stopping the motors, I had to cut a few wires. You only need to reconnect them, and everything will work properly again W.
Ten thousand thundering typhoons! He has gone out into space to save our lives!... And I accused him...
Yes, Captain. But even so, perhaps his sacrifice will be in vain... You go on up. I'll just repair these wires...
Ah, there you are. Well, have you caught that thug Wolff?
?
What? What did you say? Wolff a thug?! If ever I hear you say one disrespectful thing about that hero, I'll throw you into space to join him! You understand, you iconoclast, you?!
At that moment...
Earth to Moon-Rocket... Stand by... Ten minutes to go before the turning operation.
Right.
A quarter of an hour later...
Earth to Moon-Rocket... Turning operation successfully accomplished. Don't give in! In less than two hours you will be back on the Earth.
Yes!... And they'll give us an impressive memorial! I can see it from here! To Captain Haddock, a martyr in the cause of Science, etcetera, etcetera!
Well, if I have to die, then at least let it be in the way I choose, blistering barnacles!
Captain! What are you going to do?

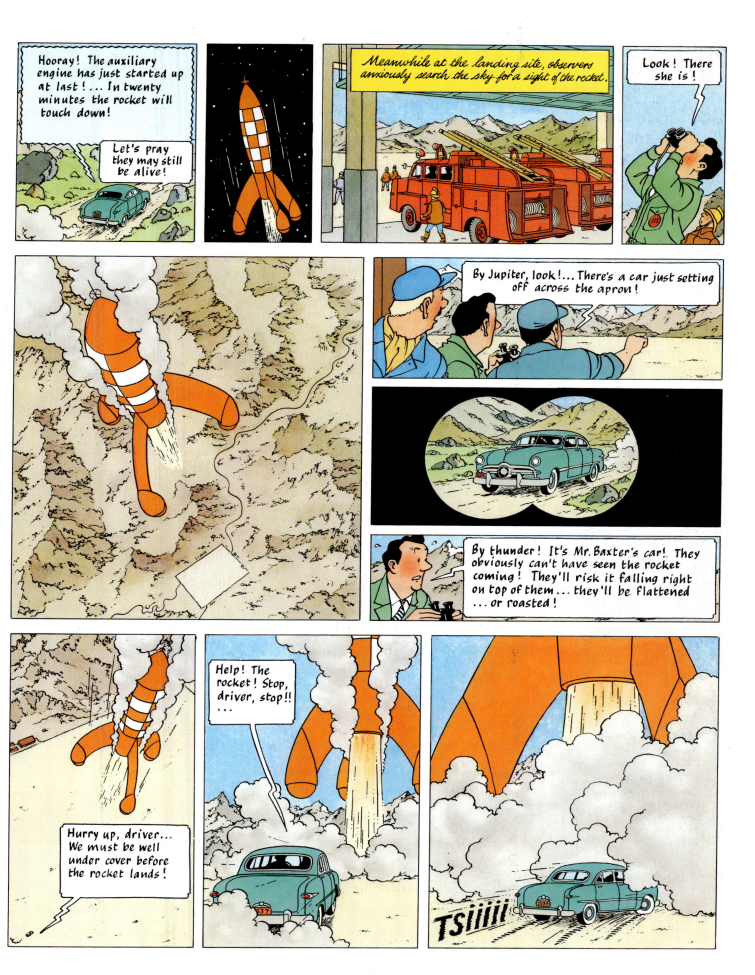

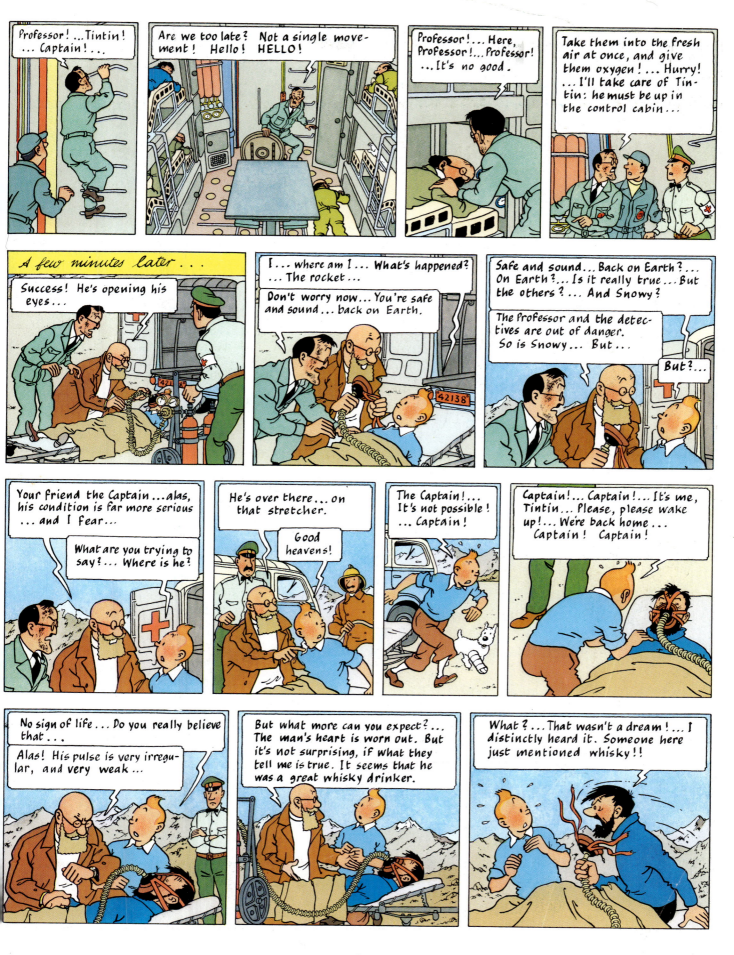

THE END